Aurora Cáceres

A DEAD ROSE

Translation, foreword & notes
Laura Kanost

- STOCKCERO -

Translation, Foreword, bibliography & notes © Laura Kanost
of this edition © Stockcero 2018
1st. Stockcero edition: 2018

ISBN: 978-1-934768-95-2

Library of Congress Control Number: 2018941915

Set in Linotype Granjon font family typeface
Printed in the United States of America on acid-free paper.

Published by Stockcero, Inc.
3785 N.W. 82nd Avenue
Doral, FL 33166
USA
stockcero@stockcero.com

www.stockcero.com

Aurora Cáceres

A Dead Rose

Contents

Translator's Introduction

In 1909, Zoila Aurora Cáceres (1877-1958) stated in her book *Mujeres de ayer y de hoy* [Women of Yesterday and Today] that most women writers "are not creators, nor do they impress upon the art of literature the wholesome, benevolent hallmark that ought to characterize every woman." She went on: "In general, feminine novels do not differ from those written by men: they are just as audacious, pornographic, impetuous, and passionate as those produced by the masculine pen" (343-44).[1] It sounds like condemnation, but five years later, in her own novel *La rosa muerta* (*A Dead Rose*), Cáceres pulled out all the stops. She dared to write a detailed account of a uterine ailment and a sexual relationship between a woman and her gynecologist. Defying cultural conventions of feminine modesty to speak openly about women's health and sexuality is only part of what made this novel scandalous, however. Just as audacious was the way Cáceres positioned her novel within an artistic context that silenced women.

Planting her work firmly within a Spanish American *modernista* tradition of male artists obsessed with perfect forms that objectified women as muses or *femmes fatales*, Zoila Aurora Cáceres fashioned a female character who plays all of those roles. Her protagonist, Laura (whose name happens to overlap with the author's, *Zoi–LA a–U–ro–RA*), is an artist who has created a stylized, perfect form –her body– that harbors a hidden threat. Ultimately, this artist embraces her inner *femme fatale* even though it means confronting death, and in doing

---

1   "Salvo raros casos, no son creadoras, ni imponen al arte literario el sello sano y benévolo que debería caracterizar a toda mujer; no revelan un temperamento que emane de las bondades y ternuras de su alma. Por lo general, las novelas femeninas no difieren de las que escriben los hombres: son tan osadas, pornográficas, impetuosas y apasionadas como las que produce la pluma masculina." All translations are my own unless otherwise noted.

so she chooses to destroy her perfect work of art, leaving only copies in the form of painting and sculpture. In conflating the artist, the work, the muse, and the *femme fatale*, Cáceres signaled the impossibility of writing as a woman within the discourse of *modernismo* even as she did just that. As she narrated gynecological treatment and sexual encounters from Laura's vantage point, Cáceres rewrote naturalist and positivist scripts that objectified women's bodies as laboratory specimens and sites of social control. She defied sociocultural restrictions on women's sexuality, as well as artistic expectations – which she herself had voiced in [Women of Yesterday and Today]– that women writers should imbue their work with their delicate spirits.

Why did Cáceres dare to write *A Dead Rose*, a book so scandalous that nearly a century went by before it saw a second edition? The novel must have come as a shock to many of the readers who had followed Cáceres's earlier writings, often published under her pseudonym, Evangelina or Eva Angelina (evoking the gospels or *evangelios*) or with her initials, ZAC. In many ways, however, *A Dead Rose* is an extension of Cáceres's cosmopolitan identity and feminist stance developed over a lifetime of travel and scholarship.

As the daughter of Andrés Avelino Cáceres, the Peruvian president (1886-1890, 1894-1895) known for his military leadership in the War of the Pacific (1879-1883), young Aurora spent much of her childhood on the move. Her mother, Antonia Moreno, took her three daughters along with her as she bravely provided support for her husband's troops fighting against the Chilean invasion, and the family was exiled to Argentina when her father's first presidency ended in a coup (Pachas Maceda 21-25). The family's social position allowed Aurora to devote her time to learning, writing, and developing her social network. Illustrating this privilege, in July 1906 diary entries from her autobiography, Cáceres complains about picking up a broom to sweep the floor for the first time in her life, as she has not yet been able to hire a servant for her new household (*Mi vida* 101). Aurora's parents sent her to the best schools, not only in Peru, but also England, Germany, and France, where she developed a love of art and multilingual skills that she would later apply as a literary translator. The character Laura in *A Dead Rose* shares a similar education and knowledge of painting (Pachas Maceda 90-91).

Cáceres developed a broad social and intellectual network, publishing essays and stories in a multitude of periodicals on both sides of the Atlantic. Fellow Peruvian Clorinda Matto de Turner, who was exiled in Argentina at the same time as the Cáceres family, published Evangelina's early feminist essay "La emancipación de la mujer" (The Emancipation of Woman, 1896) in an early issue of her publication *Búcaro Americano*. An argument in favor of women's education in this early essay –"How much nicer would it be for a man to find in his companion, not an ignorant being for whom he must seek light conversation within her comprehension, but a woman whose intellect is on his level, a woman with whom he could share all the troubles of his soul, future projects, present fears or joys?"[2] (Glickman 106)– reappears nearly two decades later in *A Dead Rose*, in an explanation of how Laura's lover, Dr. Castel, grew distanced from his wife: "the young woman's frivolity distanced her intellectually from her husband, and with that moral remoteness, physical detachment soon followed."

Beginning in about 1902, Cáceres spent much of her time in Europe. She completed studies at the Sorbonne culminating in a thesis on feminism in Berlin, accompanied her father on diplomatic travels in Europe, and visited her sister Hortensia, who lived in Paris (Pachas Maceda 28). In 1905, she combined a European model with her extensive Peruvian social network to found the Centro Social de Señoras in Peru, promoting women's vocational education and supporting child development to, in her words, "expand woman's field of action, emancipating her from the needle" (Araujo 174-75).[3]

In the Spanish illustrated periodical *Álbum Salón* in 1902, Emilia Serrano, Baronesa de Wilson included Cáceres in her series "Inmortales americanas," paying homage to nine great women of the Americas including writers Mercedes Cabello de Carbonera and Soledad Acosta de Samper. Accompanied by a photograph, the tribute presents Cáceres as a beautiful, very young woman whose admirable intellect developed at the incredibly rapid new pace of

---

2   "¿Cuánto más agradable no sería para un hombre encontrar en su compañera, en vez del ser ignorante, para con el cual tiene que buscar conversaciones frívolas que le sean comprensibles, a una mujer cuyo intelectual le haya puesto a su altura, es decir, con la que pueda compartir todas las cuitas de su alma, proyectos para el porvenir, temores o alegrías del presente?"

3   "abrir campo de acción a la mujer emancipándola de la aguja"

modern life, and whose writing in several Spanish American periodicals on topics including psychology, law, science, art, and literature quickly gained admirers due to her skill for observation and "the most exquisite, most pure sentiment."[4] This assessment, like Amado Nervo's later prologue for *A Dead Rose*, dovetails with the expectation for "poetisas" or poetesses of the time to write "'intimist' verse about matters of the heart", poetry that was "emotive but self-abnegating, devoid of excessive passion, and expressive of 'feminine' qualities of gentleness, softness, purity, beauty, fragility, and moral superiority" (Unruh 42). But the Baronesa de Wilson goes further, praising Evangelina's curiosity and perceptive treatment of "social and sensational problems."[5] The essay reinforces Cáceres's image as a cosmopolitan intellectual, characterizing her as "American by birth and European by her deep, expansive education."[6]

Cáceres's personal album includes clippings of two 1903 profiles in the Argentine publication *América Literaria*, both accompanied by photographic portraits. One, signed "Saint Just," celebrates Cáceres's rapid rise to stardom as an example of what women can achieve when they have access to education, quoting from the essay by the Baronesa de Wilson. Another, signed "R.B.S.," praises the artistic merit and prodigious imagination of Cáceres's publications, as well as her modesty. Like the 1902 feature, this one goes beyond complimenting the "feminine" features of Cáceres's writing: "We know that she works hard; she studies more; she has penned pages of profound sentiment in which a woman's heart beats with every pulse of a man's!"[7] This writer emphasizes the role of Cáceres's experiences of war and exile in shaping her intelligence, sure to produce "treasures of beauty yet to be discovered."[8] In her many visual portraits (three sketches, three oil paintings, and a sculpture, plus numerous photographs) Cáceres cultivated a stylized image of an elegant, confident woman (see Pachas Maceda).

Cáceres's literary network put her in touch with famed Guatemalan *modernista* writer Enrique Gómez Carrillo, and they ex-

---

4   "el sentimiento más exquisito y más puro"
5   "los problemas sociales y sensacionales"
6   "americana por su nacimiento y europea por lo profundo y vasto de su educación"
7   "Sabemos que trabaja mucho; que estudia más; que tiene páginas de un sentimiento profundo en que palpita un corazón de muger con todas las pulsaciones de un hombre!"
8   "tesoros de belleza no descubiertos todavía"

changed a few letters beginning in 1902 (Cáceres, *Mi vida* 11). Her au-
tobiographical account of her life with Gómez Carrillo begins with
a 1902 diary entry in which her first letter from Gómez Carrillo reminds her of the time she secretly read his sordid novel *Del amor, del
dolor y del vicio* [Of Love, Of Pain, and Of Vice]; although she is not
impressed by the style of his enclosed portrait, she imagines that conversation with such an intelligent young writer must be much more
entertaining than speaking with the young men of her social circle
(*Mi vida* 11-13). In entries dated 1906, Cáceres discusses her "ob-
session" with Gómez Carrillo's writing (*Mi vida* 15) and her gratitude
to the Baronesa de Wilson for mentioning to Gómez Carrillo that
Cáceres had just arrived in Paris and encouraging him to contact her
(*Mi vida* 22). In *Mi vida con Enrique Gómez Carrillo* [My Life with Enrique Gómez Carrillo] (1929), Cáceres presents diary entries and
letters to portray the mutual intellectual admiration that sparked their
troubled romance (Miseres 410): "No one has understood me better
than he has by treating me like a writer and not like a society lady,
because if I love anything in life it is the literary profession, which
permits one to think, feel, and say everything freely" (*Mi vida* 27).[9]
Their tumultuous marriage, which lasted from June 1906 to April
1907, would give Cáceres intimate access to *modernista* circles.

They were seen as something of an odd couple; she was a devout
Catholic, a president's daughter concerned with proper behavior and
appearance, while he was a bohemian libertine, prone to dueling and
affected by neurasthenia –a perceived weakness of the nerves thought
to be exacerbated by stress, intellectual exertion, and the rapid pace
of modern life (Simon 114-17). By Cáceres's account, although they
were in love and spent happy hours together reading and writing,
Gómez Carrillo quickly became unbearable to live with, extremely
unstable and controlling. Observing Cáceres's complaints about the
frequent presence of a certain male friend referred to only as "L.,"
Lucía Fox Lockert suggests that another aspect of this "illness" that
caused conflict in their relationship was Enrique's attraction to men,
which he discussed as "androgismo" in his own autobiography (334).
Despite Cáceres's Catholic opposition to divorce, they separated after

---

9   "Nadie me ha comprendido mejor que él al tratarme como a escritora y no como a
    señorita de sociedad, porque si algo amo en la vida es la profesión literaria, en la que es
    permitido pensar, sentir y decirlo todo libremente."

only ten months and formalized their divorce in 1922. She never re-
married.

Fewer intimate details are known about Cáceres's life after her
separation from her husband, since her published autobiography focuses on their relationship. Her activities as a lecturer, writer, and
social activist continued to draw on and develop her international
network. A 1909 article in *Caras y caretas* (Buenos Aires) on the Unión
Literaria she founded "to unite and defend the writers of Spain,
France, and Latin America"[10] praises her "aristocratic" salons. The
Unión Literaria, which included famed Spanish writers Miguel de
Unamuno and Emilia Pardo Bazán, supported authors' rights, translation, and the international dissemination of literary production. In
1911, Cáceres organized the first telephone operator union in Peru
and started, also in Peru, the Society for the Protection of Fine Arts
and Historical Monuments (Sociedad Protectora de Bellas Artes y
Monumentos Históricos); in 1915, she led the Lima Catholic
Women's Union (Unión Católica de Señoras de Lima) (Araujo 175).
In 1909 Cáceres wrote, "What truly characterizes our epoch, what is
truly new about it, is the mass uprising, the common ambition, the
organization of groups and societies, and their strength and com-
munion of aspirations, which extend beyond national borders to con-
stitute an international power [...] A feminist woman is never a for-
eigner; in any great capital where she sets foot, she will find the
welcome of a society and the attention of her colleagues" (*Mujeres de
ayer* 341).[11]

Her books *Mujeres de ayer y de hoy* [Women of Yesterday and
Today] (1909) and *Oasis de arte* [Art Oasis] (1911?), published in Paris,
display her wide social network, encyclopedic knowledge, extensive
travels, and passion for women's education –which, Cáceres argued,
did not conflict with the revered role of mother. [Women of Yesterday
and Today] is an ambitious work aiming to compare the roles of
women in various cultures and time periods and their educational,
legal, and political systems; it recounts the accomplishments of

---

10   "para la unión y defensa de los escritores de España, Francia y América Latina"
11   "En verdad, lo que caracteriza nuestra época, lo que tiene de verdaderamente nuevo,
     es el levantamiento en masa, la ambición común, la organización de grupos y socieda-
     des, y su fuerza y comunión de aspiraciones, que traspasa los límites de la patria para
     constituir un poder internacional [...] Una feminista no es una extranjera, en cualquiera
     gran capital adonde llegue, encontrará la buena acogida de una sociedad y la solicitud
     de sus colegas"

women leaders, writers, and other notable figures, drawing connections to present-day feminism. Then it focuses on numerous present-day women intellectuals and feminists from both sides of the Atlantic, including details apparently gleaned from personal connections and a discussion of Cáceres's own work with the Centro Social de Señoras.

Several ideas from [Women of Yesterday and Today] reappear in *A Dead Rose*. Dr. Castel's opinion that "the most beautiful women have the least talent and soul; the banality of their thoughts generally makes them unbearable" and preference for "eyes that speak not in trifles, but in the language of intelligence" echo Cáceres's affirmation in [Women] that "our taste in beauty has changed. For a woman to be pleasing, before beauty, she must possess spirituality and elegance. Even in painting, more than women of perfect beauty, artists prefer interesting women as their models" (216).[12] [Women] contains a lengthy, sympathetic discussion of Roman courtesans that is linked to the portrayal of Laura through comparisons to flowers and the remark that they "died young and beautiful." Cáceres describes the courtesan Imperia as "a flower of love" who "spread her intoxicating perfume, succumbing with her youth and beauty in full bloom" (*Mujeres* 114).[13] Explaining that Imperia was absolved and blessed by Julius II, Cáceres writes that "the public pardoned her for a life free as a marvelous bird, because devoting herself to love, her caresses were received as a gift. As she walked down the streets vibrant and rhythmic, testimony of the admiration she inspired surrounded her with a halo of apotheosis. After her death, she was remembered kindly 'because she knew how to die young and beautiful'" (*Mujeres* 114).[14] The sympathy Cáceres expresses for the courtesan –like Laura, a flower-like beauty with a rhythmic walk who loved freely and died young– illuminates the discrepancy Ward observed between the religious conviction Cáceres expresses in her autobiography and the lack thereof in *A Dead Rose* (vii-ix).

---

12   "nuestro gusto por la belleza ha cambiado. Para que una mujer guste, necesita antes que ser bella, ser espiritual y elegante. Aun en pintura, más que mujeres de belleza perfecta, los artistas prefieren como modelos a las mujeres interesantes"

13   "una flor de amor, esparció su perfume embriagador, para sucumbir en pleno florecimiento de juventud y hermosura"

14   "el público la perdonó su vida libre de pájaro maravilloso, porque al entregarse al amor, sus caricias eran recibidas como un don. Al pasar por las calles vibrante y rítmica, el testimonio de la admiración que causaba la rodeaba de una aureola de apoteosis. Después de muerta su recuerdo fue simpático 'porque supo morir siendo joven y bella'"

[Oasis of Art] is a collection of essays showcasing Cáceres's travels and social connections, as well as her thoughts on art, theater, and even airplanes. Its prologue by leading *modernista* Rubén Darío underscores Cáceres's uncomfortable position within *modernismo*. Darío begins by "confessing" that he isn't a fan of women writers –probably because, he says, most of them are ugly; acknowledging that writing resembling embroidery can sometimes be charming, Darío describes Cáceres as a beautiful compatriot of Santa Rosa de Lima and fills up the rest of his prologue with a list of places discussed in the book and a lengthy quotation (Ruiz Barrionuevo 31). Cáceres's assessment of Berlin as lacking both joy and sorrow (*Oasis* 285) and remarks about its aesthetically displeasing statues (*Oasis* 287-89) and the girth of German women (*Oasis* 312) are echoed in Laura's opinions in the novel.

Las perlas de Rosa [Rosa's Pearls], the second novel published within the same 1914 Paris volume as *A Dead Rose*, provides a counterpoint to Laura's Eurocentric, *modernista* world. Although the second novel contains some *modernista* motifs –jewels, luxury materials, a focus on the "exotic," decadent intellectual soirees– it primarily engages discourses of Romanticism with emphasis on *costumbrista* local color and a plot filled with ghosts, dreams, and omens. The narrator of [Rosa's Pearls] is a cultural intermediary who explains local details for a presumably unfamiliar reader and conveys a racist attitude influenced by degeneration ideology. Chapters alternate between the story of capricious, superficial Rosa –a blond, blue-eyed, lily-white Peruvian *mestiza*– and prayers for the errant characters.

Because existing scholarship on Cáceres's writing has not extensively engaged [Rosa's Pearls], which is out of print and difficult to obtain, a detailed plot overview is in order. Rosa inherited from her *mestizo* father a mysterious illness –assuaged only by the pure air and herbal remedies of Ayacucho– as well as an abundance of pearls passed down from his indigenous grandfather, the last cacique. Spoiled and frivolous young Rosa does not recognize the value of the pearls, and for amusement, she feeds them to donkeys and tosses them in the river. Concerned about status, Rosa is ashamed of her indigenous mother and treats her disrespectfully. Rosa's marathon social gatherings, with lavish feasts, music, and poetry, are attended by local male professionals and intellectuals, as well as a few women who are not above associating with a *mestiza*, including a piano teacher. Also in attendance are a black servant, and a feminine young man who goes by Elvira and gladly dances the woman's part when needed (148).[15] Rosa becomes emotionally and physically ill after her beloved Captain Manuel goes missing. At her mother's urging, Rosa attends church and prays fervently for Manuel to return, donating her pearls to make a new mantle for the Virgin. Many years later, Rosa has become an alcoholic and dies a lonely, homeless beggar. She sees a vision of the Mater Dolorosa, who buries her in pearls and then lifts her above them. The pearls thus link an unappreciated indigenous heritage, an unanswered "impure" prayer, and the idealized, suffering mother figure. Pachas Maceda observes that the two 1914 novels share their tragic endings that do not take place without first portraying strong women who fight for their happiness with the men they love (51).

The immediate context of the writing of *A Dead Rose* and the public's initial response to this work are, to my knowledge, a mystery today. While enthusiastic reviews of [Women of Yesterday and Today] appeared in various publications a few years earlier, I have been unable to find a single contemporary mention of *A Dead Rose* or [Rosa's Pearls] beyond a list of new titles published. Perhaps *A Dead Rose* was the sort of book people did not discuss in public. In some ways, *A Dead Rose* is more scandalous than Enrique Gómez Carrillo's *Del amor, del dolor y del vicio* [Of Love, Of Pain, and Of Vice], of which Cáceres wrote in a 1902 diary entry included in her autobiography: "If they knew at home that I read it, I don't know what Mama would do with me."[16] She recalls the warning from the book's owner, her brother-in-law: "This book shouldn't be read by young ladies or even married women."[17] She sneaked the book into her room and "devoured it" before he could notice it was missing (11-12).

Following *A Dead Rose* and [Rosa's Pearls], Cáceres went on to write several additional works focused on Peru. *La campaña de la Breña, memorias del Mariscal del Perú don Andrés A. Cáceres*, a historical work co-authored with her father, was published in Lima in 1921. *La ciudad del sol* (1927), narrates a journey from Arequipa to Cusco, Peru

---

15 "se prestaba gustoso a reemplazar a una dama en el baile cuando hacía falta"
16 "Si supieran en casa que la he leído, no sé lo que mamá habrá hecho conmigo"
17 "Este libro no lo deben leer señoritas ni aun señoras"

with photographic illustrations, and *La princesa Suma Tica* (1929) is
a collection of twelve stories linked by common themes of tragedy
triggered by the loss of a loved one, poverty, or violation of rules
(Pachas Maceda 54). Also in 1929, two years after her ex-husband's
death, Cáceres published [My Life with Enrique Gómez Carrillo].

Cáceres continued to leverage her social networking skills to or-
ganize multiple groups advocating for women's rights in the 1920s
and 30s. She was active in the women's suffrage movement in Peru,
publishing in the press and organizing meetings and lectures, and
leading the organization Feminismo Peruano (Pachas Maceda 64-65).
Women won the right to vote in municipal elections in Peru in 1933.
Cáceres lived to see Peruvian women finally gain citizenship in 1955,
but she was living in Spain, where she died in 1958.

A Dead Rose AND MODERNISMO

Although Cáceres is mentioned in several histories of Peruvian
literature and Peruvian feminism (Pachas Maceda 13), her literary
writing did not begin to receive extensive critical attention until re-
searchers started to uncover the contributions of women writers to
Spanish American *modernismo* in the late 1990s. Ironically, Cáceres
has gained a new wave of readers through a movement that denied
her a clear place. Renowned *modernista* writers penned forewords for
her books, but some, like Darío, carefully worded their remarks to
distance her writing from their own; Amado Nervo states in the prologue to *A Dead Rose* that women writers should stick to romance
novels because their lives revolve around love, and notes condescend-
ingly that he will refrain from offering his advice for improving her
novel, while encouraging her to continue writing.

In another layer of irony, the *modernistas* themselves wrote auda-
ciously to carve out a place for themselves as professional writers
within a changing Spanish American social structure that did not
value local writers (Kirkpatrick 20-28): "the cult of the exotic, the emphasis on sonority, the enrichment of poetic meter, the delight in
verbal play for its own sake, helped create for the *modernistas* a self-
containment for poetry, setting it off from the everyday, commu-

nicative functions of language" (Kirkpatrick 34). This turn-of-the-century movement, often demarcated by the dates 1888-1910, sought to access "the sublime through synesthetic experiments of sound, color, and rhythm" and appropriated, sometimes with "grotesque exaggeration," iconography from French Parnassianism, symbolism, and decadentism, as well as a vast array of cultures and places considered "exotic or distant" (Kirkpatrick 18). *Modernista* imagery is replete with swans, statues, flowers, jewels, luxurious rooms, and beautiful, often dangerous, women. Even though women were important consumers of *modernista* writing (Martínez), "the female figure in *modernismo* is an object almost at one with the language, heavily decorated, distant and elusive" (Kirkpatrick 8).

The *modernistas* alienated women writers not only by casting women as objects. The physical spaces of *modernista* networks (all-male clubs, bars and cafés, offices) were not accessible to "respectable" women "still fighting the belief that any woman who wanted to write was somehow 'loose' or brazen" (Frederick 30-31), so that while *modernistas* "fetishized the feminine as an image, as an aesthetic trope, and as a discourse, very few women participated as writers in the social networks that helped to define the movement" (Moody 59). Writing in 1984, Nancy Saporta Sternbach surmised, "because *modernistas* considered themselves to be a men's literary club, a fraternity, in their own words, the female writer may have purposely eschewed becoming a part of an aesthetic which destroyed women" (ix). Bonnie Frederick notes that access to education and libraries posed additional structural barriers to women's participation in the *modernista* aesthetic; "[m]oreover, the cult of beauty and art for art's sake that characterized *modernismo* must have seemed frivolous to women who were struggling to gain respect as serious intellectuals and who advocated projects of social reform" (31).

Women writers who did engage with the *modernista* aesthetic were often perceived by the shapers of the canon as beyond the movement, as part of an appendix labelled "*posmodernismo*," or more vaguely, "escritura femenina" or women's writing (Escaja 4). The contributions of women writers to *modernismo* were omitted from most literary histories and anthologies, and are still under-recognized despite new scholarship bringing them to light over the past three decades (Escaja 1-12). Robert Jay Glickman's groundbreaking anthology *Vestales del templo azul* collects *modernista* representations of women –many of them authored by men– including Cáceres's 1896 essay on the emancipation of women. A growing number of critics now recognize that poetry by women such as María Enriqueta, Delmira Agustini, Juana Borrero, and María Eugenia Vaz Ferreira, as Tina Escaja puts it, was not written from the margins but within the very heart of *modernismo* (11-12).

Modernismo influenced many women writers even though its representations of women as objects excluded them from the role of author. Cáceres's Uruguayan contemporary Delmira Agustini created a poetic voice that expressed this impossible position. In Sarah Moody's reading, through grotesque, violent images, Agustini "usurps and then reworks a rhetorical system that ostensibly excludes her as a woman"; "Agustini's poems explicitly contest the *modernista* limitation of women's role as passive object and forcibly create a space for women's writing, calling attention to the violence of the dynamic, that is, to both the violence of her own gesture and the violence of the exclusion that she would disrupt" (Moody 60).

One example of the way Agustini and other women rewrote *modernista* scripts was their representation of statues. Rather than joining the *modernista* fraternity in exalting the statue as a perfect form, Agustini's poetic speaker in "La estatua" ("The Statue," 1907) sees in the feminine statue a visceral longing to be more than an object:

> Behold it, thus –on bended knee– in imperial
> Calm, imposing frightful nakedness!
> God!... Move that body, give it a soul!
> See the greatness that sleeps in its form...
> See it up there, wretched, defenseless,
> Poorer than a worm, forever calm! (Agustini and Cáceres 36-37)[18]

The lesser known Uruguayan poet Luisa Luisi also re-envisioned the perfect statue image to voice an anguished conflict of desire and form in her 1926 poem "A la Victoria de Samotracia" ("To the Winged Victory of Samothrace"). Like Agustini, Luisi ascribes to the statue a desperate longing for motion; readers have connected Luisi's reinter-

---

18   Miradla así –de hinojos!– en augusta
      Calma imponer la desnudez que asusta!...–
      Dios!...Moved ese cuerpo, dadle un alma!
      Ved la grandeza que en su forma duerme...
      ¡Vedlo allá arriba, miserable, inerme,
      Más pobre que un gusano, siempre en calma!

pretation to the poet's own experience of paralysis:

> Oh! Victory, Victory, divine marble,
> Like me, condemned to immobility;
> All her soul set upon open wings,
> Mutilated in the supreme impetus to fly!...
>
> Yearning for movement! Yearning to rise,
> To run, to take off in masterful flight!...
> Desire, painful in its impossibility,
> To walk... to walk... to walk!...
>
> Oh, Victory, Victory of Samothrace,
> Image of my life, all immobility;
> In divine marble turned prison of flight
> Tremendous, desperate yearning to fly!..(Kanost n.p.)[19]

Cáceres was an early contributor to this *modernista* counter-discourse. Her story titled "¿Mujer o mármol?" [Woman or Marble?] appeared in *La Alborada* in 1899 (Cáceres, *Álbum personal*). The story opens with this line: "The artist fell in love with a superb form. –Was this a woman or was this marble?"[20] Obsessed with her goddess-like beauty, the artist gives up on painting, and expresses his passionate suffering in verse, to no avail: she is cold and indifferent. "Was this a woman or was this marble?," the narrator repeats throughout the story. Nearly dead, the artist is unable to break the spell of passion awoken in him by her beauty, and his tears reach the divine figure's heart. The "marble woman" ("mujer mármol") is moved to embrace the dying artist, and kisses him as he breathes his last breath. Now the Goddess of Indifference sheds two tears: "Yes, she cried, because she was a woman."[21] The story ends with the repeated question, "Was

---

19   Oh! ¡¡Victoria, Victoria, mármol divino,
     como yo condenada a la inmovilidad;
     con toda el alma puesta en las alas abiertas,
     mutilada en el ímpetu supremo de volar!...

     ¡Ansia de movimiento! ¡Anhelo de elevarse,
     de correr, de subir en vuelo magistral!...
     Deseo doloroso a fuerza de imposible
     de andar... de andar... de andar!..

     ¡Oh, Victoria, Victoria de Samotracia,
     imagen de mi vida, toda inmovilidad;
     en el mármol divino, hecho cárcel del vuelo,
     ansia desesperada, enorme, de volar!...

20   "El artista se enamoró de una forma soberbia. –¿Era mujer o mármol?"

this a woman or was this marble?," possibly asked this time by the marble woman herself. Like the later texts by Agustini and Luisi, the inability of Cáceres's beautiful marble woman to move or act is associated with suffering; in this case, both the male artist and the female object of his passion suffer. Cáceres continued to work with this motif in *A Dead Rose*, with a protagonist with marble-white skin and a perfect shape who does not break away from her own fatal passion.

Cáceres's dialogue with *modernismo* is even more noteworthy because of the scarcity of *modernista* prose authored by women. *A Dead Rose* became, in 2007, "the only readily available example of *modernista* prose by a prominent woman writer in Latin America" (LaGreca 617). Chantal Berthet's 2014 dissertation establishes a first corpus of *modernista* prose by women writers (Teresa González de Fanning, Inés Echeverría Larraín, Emma de la Barra, Aurora Cáceres and Teresa de la Parra). While very few women writers of prose positioned themselves as *modernistas*, several did engage *modernista* discourses to critique or revise them. Vicky Unruh describes an early short story by Alfonsina Storni ("La fina crueldad," 1916) in which Amalia, the protagonist, "embodies both the *modernista* aesthetic and its pristine ideal of feminine beauty. The story portrays Amalia's objectification of a female friend ... Amalia's repulsion by the realization that her friend would be even more artistically perfect were she dead signals not only her rejection of *modernismo* but also the ethical turmoil it generates in women who embrace it" (42). Unruh also reads several Magda Portal short stories of the early 1920s that "enact Portal's failure to craft her art of living as a writer within the *modernista* ethos" through women characters who "evolve from the lovelorn, submissive painter's model in 'Violetas' to the recalcitrant model in 'Mujer' who casts off her poses as rapidly as she tries them on to the vibrant, all-too-human dancer in 'El fracaso'" (174-75). Carmen Lyra blends *modernista* imagery with social critique in her 1918 novel *En una silla de ruedas* [In a Wheelchair], which imagines an alternative national family of authentic Costa Rican artists who are socially marginalized due to their non-normative bodies (Kanost). Robert McKee Irwin notes that María Luisa Garza's 1922 novel *La novia de Nervo* [Nervo's Girlfriend] aligns with *modernismo* in its "language of degeneration, the exaltation of the figure

---

21   "Sí, lloró, porque era mujer."

of Nervo, the focus on gender-related social ills, the European setting, and the transgender fantasy," but "its feminist social consciousness takes it a step beyond" (141-42).

Although women writers were marginalized by the social spaces and discourses of *modernismo*, Cáceres positioned her novel *A Dead Rose* unmistakably within this movement —Ward accurately describes it as *"hipermodernista"* (xiii). The text is brimming with *modernista* motifs: flowers, birds, marble, luxurious interior spaces such as Dr. Castel's waiting room and Laura's bedroom, elements considered "exotic," Dr. Castel's jewel-like surgical instruments, cosmopolitan settings, modern technologies such as electric lights and the pneumatic mail system, and portrayals of illness and sexuality that violate social norms. As Berthet points out, *A Dead Rose* matches key elements of the *modernista* novel identified by Aníbal González: a cosmopolitan, urban setting and an intellectual protagonist devoted to art, but unable to produce (164).

Moreover, Cáceres links her novel to *modernismo* through intertextuality. In the first chapter, she works the title of her ex-husband's novel, *Del amor, del dolor y del vicio* [Of Love, Of Pain, and Of Vice], into a sentence as a sort of literary wink. Nancy LaGreca points out the allusion, which calls attention to parallels and contrasts between the two novels: "Gómez Carrillo's and Cáceres's protagonists are both young, seductively beautiful, and extraordinarily wealthy Parisian widows who discover the infidelities of their recently deceased husbands, experience an awakening of consciousness in regard to their freedom, and rebel by embarking on a journey of erotic self-discovery" (619). In LaGreca's reading, "Cáceres's narrative seeks to fill a gap in Gómez Carrillo's textual representation of feminine sexuality" by clarifying "what was at stake for women who dared to be sexually autonomous in the early twentieth century" (620).

While *modernista* novels typically portray male artists and the women who inspire them as beautiful muses or lure them as dangerously sexual *femmes fatales*, Cáceres created a female artist whose body serves as both inspiration and threat. Laura stylizes her own form to embody the *modernista* aesthetic, and the narrative gaze compels the reader to look at her much more than at any other character. Like an artist, Laura devotes her existence to her aesthetic: "She loved her body as beauty is loved, and like a pagan she worshipped it; painstakingly she studied the aesthetic of movement, the flexibility of the line, and physical exercise, which she practiced daily under the direction of a skilled gymnast." In addition to exercise, Laura uses a corset to sculpt her body, creating a waist so tiny she resembles a flower on a stem. She selects exotic, artistic clothing to highlight her statuesque body; her pale skin is repeatedly compared to marble or ivory. She perfumes her breasts to make them even more rose-like. She prefers shoes that give her walk a certain rhythm. She is, like Turkish Dr. Castel, considered exotic; Laura is described as "Levantine" because one of her grandfathers was Arab.

If Laura embodies the *modernista* aesthetic, Dr. Castel serves as her ideal audience: "a man of good taste, capable of appreciating the beauty of her shape, the splendid lines and delicate contours with which God had favored her body." Just as women made up an important part of the *modernistas'* readership, Dr. Castel is described with words normally associated with women—delicate, selfless, motherly—and he even playfully tries on Laura's hat and veil. He calls Laura's body a work of art, and he continues to admire and desire her after seeing the secret disease that threatens to destroy its beauty, perhaps because of his faith in his own art, medicine.

Laura dies because she is unwilling to suppress her own sexuality despite warnings she should remain celibate to avoid life-threatening complications of her uterine ailment. Cáceres shields her own reputation by portraying a woman who seems to be enjoying extramarital sex but actually pays for this transgression with suffering and death—clearly announced from the outset by the novel's spoiler of a title. Causing the destruction of the artist, simultaneously the *femme fatale*, Laura adds a new layer to the script Sternbach observes in *modernista* novels by male writers: "the most celebrated female protagonist of the *modernista* novel, the femme fatale, contrary to her reputation as destroyer of men, frequently suffers a premature and often violent death at the hands of the male artist/protagonist/poet" (Sternbach ix). Rebecca Mason reads the importance Laura places on her own beauty and her artistic stylization of her own body as internalized misogyny symptomatic of a patriarchal culture that objectifies women, noting the fact that Cáceres opts not to portray the loss of Laura's beauty by narrating her death. Indeed, Laura controls her own image to the very end by forbidding doctors to leave any external mark of her illness and hiding her final medical treatments and death from Dr. Castel (just as they are hidden from the reader); she leaves behind her own narrative in the form of a letter, and a nude portrait she commissioned of her perfect body. Dr. Barrios reports that Laura's cadaver continued to inspire admiration, invoking *modernismo* through references to sculpture and the color blue: "Death robbed her of life, but not of beauty. How beautiful she looked, like a statue of Carrara marble! Sculptors came to model her Grecian profile, her hands and feet, and a painter portrayed her in white tulle and lilies like a celestial virgin. Contrasting with the pallor of her face, her sardonic smile still seemed to say: I belong to the blue, to the intangible, I have left the Carnival of life!"

The novel's conclusion replaces Laura —a self-destructing conflation of *modernista* motifs— with a new woman intellectual in the form of Dr. Castel's beautiful, intelligent young daughter (LaGreca 624). Cáceres hammers home this point by having Miss Castel switch on the electric light for the older men who have been sitting around in the dark, then ending the novel by explicitly stating that Miss Castel has taken Laura's place: "no sooner does one rose lose its petals and cease to perfume one man's existence, but a new bud opens into a new blossom, just as intense as that dead rose before it." The sudden appearance of Miss Castel to take Laura's place at the end of the novel foregrounds the lack of women in Laura's story: Miss Castel is the only other female character who speaks in the novel. Laura lacks the sort of feminist support network celebrated by Cáceres; Laura's friendships with other women are mentioned only in the context of envy and competition. Cáceres signals the lack of discursive and social structures in which a female *modernista* writer could thrive.

In addition to this critique of *modernismo*, *A Dead Rose* participates in Spanish American women writers' engagement of the positivist thought underlying discourses of social hygiene and literary naturalism. Referring to writers like Juana Manuela Gorriti in 1880s Argentina, Francine Masiello observes, "Responding to the style of scrutiny and observation belonging to scientific inquiry [...] women writers overturn this discourse with personal meditations on the female body and ably question the modes of modernity put in place by leaders of the nation" (7). As Ward points out, Gorriti's 1876 *Peregrinaciones de una alma triste* [Peregrinations of a Sorrowful Soul] is a clear intertext of *A Dead Rose*: Gorriti's protagonist –named Laura– also travels to seek relief from illness, and Cáceres even uses the word "peregrinación" to describe her protagonist's search for a doctor able to cure her. In Gorriti's novel, however, as Ward observes, the protagonist finds health by traveling and ignoring doctors' advice (xviii-xix, xxii). Naturalism, according to Gabriela Nouzeilles, reproduced the power dynamic of the clinical case through an authoritative narrative gaze interpreting socially marginal bodies, while canonical *modernista* representations of illness tend to be narrated by writer figures viewing their own illnesses, so that illness generates artistic activity (149-51). Perhaps in an effort to distance what could be perceived by readers as her own voice from the transgressive experiences of her protagonist, Cáceres chooses a third-person narrator for her novel; her protagonist has deep misgivings about the motivations and effectiveness of doctors.

Cáceres includes some elements of positivism in her portrayal of Laura's illness, but science and progress are juxtaposed with descriptions of personal suffering. The origin of Laura's illness can't be known, Dr. Barrios tells her, which LaGreca reads as an insinuation that Laura's fibroids are the result of a sexually transmitted infection contracted from her unfaithful husband (620). Cáceres narrates not only the physical pain and bleeding related to Laura's condition, but also her anxiety, depression, and insomnia, and the socially conditioned humiliation she feels about undergoing gynecological examinations, particularly when being treated like "rotten meat" by Dr. Blumen in a depiction LaGreca likens to a rape scene (622). LaGreca reads Laura's refusal to obey Dr. Blumen's rules as a feminist rejection of "the patriarchal space of control over the female body" (620). Butcher-like Dr. Blumen's grotesque, filthy office contrasts with Dr. Castel's sparkling examining room, but even Dr. Castel fails to cure Laura. Cáceres's portrayal of Laura's illness considers its social, physical, and psychological dimensions, and dares to include Laura's perspective on experiences rarely given detailed literary representation—a pelvic exam, uterine hemorrhaging, a panic attack.

Unlike most Spanish American literary representations of illness of the time, Laura's illness is not reduced to a clinical case, an example of degeneration, or a symbol of social ills –nor does it merely signal the social deviance of the *modernista* intellectual or the beauty ascribed to the objectified *modernista* woman, seen as still more beautiful if languishing or dead. Rather, her illness is portrayed as a multifaceted experience that is affected by the social context within which it takes place and ultimately is not overcome through modern medicine.

This Translation

Translating this novel involved constant grappling with the changes in language and its context since 1914. I chose to maintain words referring to specific fashions and technologies of the moment, which may be unfamiliar to contemporary readers but are easily clarified by a quick internet or dictionary search. Less readily identified references are discussed in footnotes. In the case of words still in use whose meanings have changed over time (such as *promiscuo* or *holocausto* and their English cognates), however, I avoid confusion by substituting a contemporary synonym. Although Cáceres's long, convoluted sentences push the limits of acceptable style in English, I resist dividing them in order to suggest, as much as possible, her chosen structures. Likewise, to maintain the cultural context, I maintain exoticizing language ("Oriental," "Levantine," etc.) even though contemporary readers will find it racist.

As a reader, Cáceres could not stand translations, she wrote, because she disliked literary "intermediaries" and was able to read in multiple languages (*Mi vida* 76). Nevertheless, she frequently applied her multilingual skills as a translator herself, and her Unión Literaria advocated for translation as a way to increase the international reach of literature. I think Cáceres, who celebrated international feminist networks, would be pleased to know that her novel was finding its way to a new Anglophone audience, and amused to know that its translator happened to be named Laura.

Works Cited

Agustini, Delmira. *Selected Poetry of Delmira Agustini: Poetics of Eros*. Translated by Alejandro Cáceres. SIU Press, 2008.

Araujo, Kathya. "Feminista, burguesa y católica. Zoila Aurora Cáceres y las tensiones en la configuración de la mujer y lo femenino en el cambio de siglo." *Dignos de su arte: sujeto y lazo social en el Perú de las primeras décadas del siglo XX*. Iberoamericana, 2009, pp. 167-226.

Berthet, Chantal. *Body, Gender, and Nation: Women Fiction Writers of Spanish American Modernismo [Mujer, cuerpo y nación: las narradoras del modernismo]*. Dissertation, University of Connecticut, 2014. http://opencommons.uconn.edu/cgi/viewcontent.cgi?article=6825&context=dissertations

Cáceres, Zoila Aurora (Evangelina, Eva Angelina). *Álbum personal de Zoila Aurora Cáceres*. Pontificia Universidad Católica del Perú. http://repositorio.pucp.edu.pe/index/handle/123456789/64206

_____. *La campaña de la Breña, memorias del Mariscal del Perú don Andrés A. Cáceres*. Imprenta Americana, 1921. https://catalog.hathitrust.org/Record/008304548

_____. *La ciudad del sol*. Libería francesa científica y casa editorial E. Rosay, F. y E. Rosay, 1927.

_____. "La emancipación de la mujer," 1896. Robert Jay Glickman, *Vestales del templo azul. Notas sobre el feminismo hispanoamericano en la época modernista*. Canadian Academy of the Arts, 1996, pp. 104-107.

_____. *Mi vida con Enrique Gómez Carrillo*. Tipografía Nacional, 2008.

_____. *Mujeres de ayer y de hoy*. Garnier Hermanos, 1909. https://catalog.hathitrust.org/Record/101231454

_____. *Oasis de arte*. Garnier Hermanos, 1911(?). https://catalog.hathitrust.org/Record/006523305

_____. *La princesa Suma Tica*. Mundo Latino, 1929.

_____. *La rosa muerta*. Edited by Thomas Ward, Stockcero, 2007.

_____. *La rosa muerta. Las perlas de Rosa*. Garnier Hermanos, 1914.

Escaja, Tina. *Salomé decapitada: Delmira Agustini y la estética finisecular de la fragmentación*. Rodopi, 2001.

Fox Lockert, Lucía. "Dialéctica en la subversión de los sexos (La autobiografía de Aurora Cáceres)." *La ansiedad autorial. Formación de la autoría femenina en América Latina: Los textos autobiográficos*. Edited by Márgara Russotto. Equinoccio, 2006, pp. 329-342.

Frederick, Bonnie. *Wily Modesty: Argentine Women Writers, 1860-1910*. ASU Center for Latin American Studies Press, 1998.

Glickman, Robert Jay. *Vestales del templo azul. Notas sobre el feminismo Hispanoamericano en la época modernista*. Canadian Academy of the Arts, 1996.

Irwin, Robert McKee. *Mexican Masculinities*. University of Minnesota Press, 2003.

Kanost, Laura. "Mobility and the Modern Intellectual: Translated Images from Early 20th Century Literary Works in Spanish by Carmen Lyra and Luisa Luisi". *Disability Studies Quarterly*, vol. 38, no. 1, 2018, n.p. http://dx.doi.org/10.18061/dsq.v38i1.5861

Kirkpatrick, Gwen. *The Dissonant Legacy of* Modernismo: *Lugones, Herrera y Reissig, and the Voices of Modern Spanish American Poetry*. University of California Press, 1989.

LaGreca, Nancy. "Intertextual Sexual Politics: Illness and Desire in Enrique Gómez Carrillo's *Del amor, del dolor y del vicio* and Aurora Cáceres's *La rosa muerta. Hispania* vol. 95, no. 4, December 2012, pp. 617-628

Luisi, Luisa. *Poemas de la inmovilidad y Canciones al sol*. Cervantes, 1926. http://www.autoresdeluruguay.uy/biblioteca/luisa_luisi/

Martínez, José María. "El público femenino del modernismo: De la lectora figurada a la Lectora histórica en las prosas de Gutiérrez Nájera." *Revista Iberoamericana*, vol. LXVII, no. 194-195, 2001, pp. 15-29.

Masiello, Francine. *Between Civilization and Barbarism: Women, Nation, and Literary Culture in Modern Argentina*. University of Nebraska Press, 1992.

Mason, Rebecca. "Destierro, descontrol y distorsión del cuerpo femenino en *La rosa muerta* de Aurora Cáceres." *Hispanic Poetry Review* vol. 9, no. 2, 2012, pp. 63-77.

Miseres, Vanesa. "Modernismo puertas adentro: género, escritura y experiencia urbana en *Mi vida con Enrique Gómez Carrillo* de Aurora Cáceres." *MLN* 131, 2016, pp. 398–418.

Moody, Sarah T. "Radical Metrics and Feminist Modernism: Agustini Rewrites Darío's *Prosas profanas*." *Chasqui*, vol. 43, no. 1, 2014, pp. 57-67.

Nouzeilles, Gabriela. "Narrar el cuerpo propio. Retórica modernista de la enfermedad." *Estudios* vol. 9, 1997, pp. 149-76.

Pachas Maceda, Sofía. *Aurora Cáceres "Evangelina": Sus escritos sobre arte peruano*. Seminario de Historia Rural Andina, 2009.

Ruiz Barrionuevo, Carmen. "Aurora Cáceres, 'Evangelina', entre el modernismo finisecular y la reivindicación feminista." *Inti* no. 67/68, 2008, pp. 27-44.

Serrano, Emilia, Baronesa de Wilson. "Inmortales americanas. Zoila Aurora Cáceres (Evangelina)." *Álbum Salón*, January 1902, p. 257. http://hemerotecadigital.bne.es/issue.vm?id=0001464380&page=259

Simon, Linda. *Dark Light: Electricity and Anxiety from the Telegraph to the X-Ray*. Harcourt, 2004.

Soiza Reilly, Juan José. "La Unión Literaria— Su fundadora." *Caras y caretas*, 14 August 1909, no. 567, p. 82 http://hemerotecadigital.bne.es/issue.vm?id=0004293892&page=82

Sternbach, Nancy Saporta. *The Death of a Beautiful Woman: The Femme Fatale in the Spanish-American "Modernista" Novel (Dominici, Venezuela; Halmar, Chile; Larreta, Argentina)*. Dissertation, University of Arizona, 1984.

Unruh, Vicky. *Performing Women and Modern Literary Culture in Latin America: Intervening Acts*. University of Texas Press, 2006.

Ward, Thomas. "Introducción." *La rosa muerta* by Zoila Aurora Cáceres, 1914, Stockcero, 2007, pp. vii-xxiv.

Prologue by Amado Nervo

I believe that women with a divine calling to follow the errant path of letters should devote themselves to writing novels, especially novels of love. By nature, man is polygamous and woman is monogamous. Now then, polygamy and love –Christian love, at least– are unrelated; has it not been said, perchance, that love is the egoism of two? No one would think to call love the egoism of four... or five!

Man –particularly modern man– continues to understand love in a rather old-fashioned way, that is, as a simple natural function, more or less idealized by art and poetry. For woman, in contrast, unless she is aberrant, love constitutes the fundamental purpose of life. It should lead to marriage, or in any case, to the tranquility of complete possession. On the other hand, since woman is so instinctive, she possesses superior knowledge of love's every contour and detail; in woman's guile, which is likewise quite superior to masculine guile, she is content to follow the footpaths of love, rather than taking the king's highway. For all of these reasons, and others lost among the steel bars of my typewriter, woman is the ideal writer of love novels or stories. Englishwomen have understood this very well, and in Old England, love novels written by men are scarcely published these days; men concentrate, if you will, on starring in them, which is something else... and those men who do feel called to write opt for the sciences, history, criticism, etc.

In Spain and Spanish America, there are few women novelists, because there are few women intellectuals. Religious concerns and the mockery that certain people make of women writers must contribute to this in some small part; nevertheless, Emilia Pardo Bazán has produced a veritable library of novels, and Blanca de los Ríos has several imaginative books with polished style, great lexical fertility, and an expert eye for observation.

How, then, could Mrs. Aurora Cáceres's good intention to write a novel not draw applause? She is more than familiar with Paris, this "Mecca" of our ingenuous Spanish American souls; she allows herself to be penetrated by this atmosphere which is so propitious for the work of the spirit, and in the rather motley cosmopolitanism of the great *civitas* she spots interesting types with whom we cannot but sympathize after a few pages: her Spanish Laura, deliciously Parisianized, and that Oriental doctor; they fall in love amid the décor of a white clinic smelling of disinfectant; they possess one another upon a nickel operating table, and there, where the cry of unsparing human pain has so often resounded, they can be heard crying out in sensuous love, which perhaps is but another sort of pain, the greatest on earth... But Laura is ill, with an ailment that Aurora Cáceres describes fearlessly (revealing a certain study, a certain clinical eye which –alas!– doctors often lack), and with the laudable modesty of her sad flesh, she stifles her cries when possession hurts her, and sensing that the doctor (who treated her before becoming her lover) will realize the progression of the disease and perhaps feel repulsed by her, the poor heroine runs far away to hide her misery, going to a clinic in Berlin to die, leaving her beloved a delicate letter of romantic feminism:

> *"Forgive me for hiding so much from you, and for preferring in my womanly vanity to die abroad, far from you, rather than leave you with the image of my mutilated, wrecked body associated with the memory of our love. I have said nothing to you of the physical pains that have come over me during our hours of love; the improvement I always spoke of was a lie, as were my happiness and laughter. Only my love was true, and the only thing that was indestructible was this passion, so intense that it burns my soul and overflows from my chest, such that the world would seem a small audience to hear me proclaim it.*
> *I wanted my love to brighten your existence, for my youthful soul like a fragrant incarnate flower to delight your eyes, weary of the sight of suffering; but today, as my adverse destiny transforms me from an astonishing Venus –as you used to call me– into sad hospital waste, annihilated and exhausted, I prefer to run away, to distance myself from you and thus await my death... at least I will leave you the memory of the mysterious woman of the Bosphorus, 'with tresses of seagrass and eyes of the Oriental night,' and not the painful picture of my dying moments amid bandages, chloroform, and bloody scalpels."*

***

These lovely novels of male doctors and female patients are favored now, one might say. I recently read one in the *El Temps* feuilleton that had been translated from German; its author's name is Hans Land and its protagonist is a great surgeon of Berlin: Arthur Imhoff. I recommend this novel, lovely in every way, to 50-year-old men who intend to marry 18-year-old girls... It will be instructive!...

As for Mrs. Cáceres's little book, I could perhaps quibble with certain syntactical constructions, or vocabulary that is rather cosmopolitan... like the protagonists, or the sudden intrusion of some crude naturalist detail that is no longer in style, perhaps for good reason; but I understand that my distinguished and kind friend, doing me the honor of requesting a few lines by way of a prologue for her book, does not precisely desire criticism. That will arrive by other channels than this, and I hope it does come, so that the book endures and the novelist feels stimulated to create new works as worthy as this one.

That said, after offering the author *tous mes hommages*, "to my solitudes I go," as another man said.

A Dead Rose

Chapter I

Laura slowly ascended the staircase to the second floor of a beautiful house in Paris. The stony bluish pallor of her marble-white face accentuated the shadow of large violet circles beneath her dark, almond-shaped eyes. Her bright, commanding gaze seemed tempered by an expression of immense sorrow. Her full lips, reddened with carmine, smiled timidly, the dissembling smile of the fearful, threatening to dissolve into a pained grimace...

The staircase was not steep, nor were the stairs tall; wide steps covered by a plush carpet offered the visitor a comfortable ascent. Laura climbed slowly, striving in vain to conceal the breathlessness weighing on her chest as though her heart were being torn out. Her heart was beating so violently that she stopped for a moment to catch her breath; then she continued slowly on her way, the swishing fluid silk of her dress rustling gently next to her body.

Suddenly uneasy, as though caught off guard, she stopped on the second floor and fixed her eyes upon the door through which she must pass; she was paralyzed with terror at the prospect that her fate would be sealed there in but a few short moments.

This would be her final dolorous excursion; she did not wish to suffer any additional shame or disappointment; there, in that tormented chamber of joy and pain, science and art, life and death, her destiny would be determined when that door opened, breaking a silence that concealed, like a human mystery, something of love, of pain, and of vice —when she was granted entrance to the dwelling she had designated as the final refuge for her woes.

She had to summon the last remaining energy sustaining her after many hours of indescribable sorrow, to go through with ringing the bell which shone impertinently upon the dark wood like a golden bud.

A servant, a courteous young man with curly hair and a kind face, ushered her attentively into a small waiting room, which without appearing luxurious, nevertheless denoted the prosperity of the man of the house. There were velvety oriental carpets, large Louis XVI-style armchairs, Aubusson tapestry divans and chairs, quilted silk curtains in time-worn hues, and Japanese porcelain adorning a modern bargueño cabinet. No detail betrayed a personal taste, nor did the smallest object suggest the hand of a woman.

Chapter II

Her voice trembling, Laura asked the servant, "May I see the doctor?"

He replied, "Please wait a moment, madam. The doctor is out, but he will return without delay. Your appointment begins at two o'-clock, which is in just a few minutes." He then disappeared, quickly shutting a tall white door with gilded stucco and trim.

Laura checked her watch: she had fifteen minutes left to wait. She looked at herself in the hearth mirror across from her, seeking her image in the small spaces between a colossal pendulum and heavy china lamps serving as vases.

Her beautiful classical features were poorly disguised by the black veil fitted to her hat. Far from extinguished, the dazzling brilliance of her eyes produced a mysterious charm. She concealed her body in an ample otter-fur coat that covered her down to her feet, and her *musume* hands were ensconced in a large muff of the same material. Leaning back comfortably in an armchair, her body rested, while her soul was anxious.

In vain, she endeavored to contain her restlessness.

She saw her past play out before her with the force of the present moment. She recalled her peregrination of pain through the clinics of Berlin. It was a pilgrimage of sacrifice, of slaughter. She still shivered in terror at the vision of that first day, not long ago, when a physician told her: "Take care of yourself, madam; what you have may be serious."

***

Was it possible in the space of a few weeks to live the tragedy of existence and its infinite anguish in dark solitude?

"This burden is cruel, it's inhuman," she longed to shout, but the pride of her blood rose up like a furious sea, signaling that sorrow must keep silent.

Spring came to an end, and with jubilation, Paris felt the first warmth after a winter of rain and inclement storms.

At the house of a female friend late one afternoon, Laura had seen Dr. Barrios, a compatriot of hers who, if he did not enjoy a reputation as a great doctor, had instead great fame for being frank, a good friend, a man of conscience, a scrupulous professional, and a ladies' man true to his race.

It was a hot, summery evening with light as clear as crystal and love in the air.

The last tea of the season was taking place at the home of Mrs. D... All were in agreement that the time had come to close the salons and gather in the Bois under the shade of the green and white blossoming chestnut trees, to hear the languid music of the gypsies under the open sky.

Dr. Barrios walked over to Laura and looked about, and once he was convinced that they were among people who did not understand Spanish, he began to speak with exuberant loquacity, unconcerned with those nearby.

That day, Laura was wearing an elegant hand-embroidered batiste ensemble with Venetian lace insets and foam-light Valencian ruffles, over a soft rose-colored satin slip that was fitted to her body, lending a daring nude appearance. She was not unaware that she had the impeccable contours of a Venus, and she took advantage of fashion's permissiveness to display her statuesque Levantine figure.

"That waist!," Dr. Barrios exclaimed when he caught sight of her as a ray of sunlight illuminated their nook under the canopy of a languishing palm tree. Dr. Barrios believed it polite to direct a compliment to Laura, having kept her for some time, recounting a recent romantic escapade.

Laura would often say, "I can divide my male friends into two categories: those who fall in love with me and those who tell me about their love lives." On this occasion, she was not mistaken: Dr. Barrios was of the second sort; he confided in her. A single utterance from

Laura was enough: "Doctor, what is it? You're happier than usual today."

"You bet I'm happy, with good reason. I've never been one to have a romance with a female patient, never wanting to mix professional affairs with love, but it so happens that a female friend of mine has become my patient. I met her at a ball at the Élysée. I didn't know who she was... One day, after meeting a few times, she didn't attend as planned, and she sent me a pneumatic letter.[22]

"The poor thing was ill, and she was asking me to go see her, in the capacity of physician. Imagine my surprise: she was married to a respectable judge, who showered me with attention. That day I learned her true name for the first time. What misfortune! She has been seriously ill, it could not be more serious. There she was, dying, and me by her side, spending entire nights without sleeping, seeing that I was losing her, that science was useless. You can't imagine, Laura, how horrible it is for a doctor to sense a loved one's life slipping away. Fortunately, my fears are allayed now: all danger has passed. It's as though I, too, have come back to life along with her. Now you see I have reason to rejoice, which is why I look so happy."

"The husband, too?" Laura said innocently, grinning like a mischievous schoolgirl.

"Of course!" Dr. Barrios replied ingenuously...

After unleashing his effusive spirit, Dr. Barrios paused and looked searchingly at Laura's body, no doubt because of the tightness of her corset. Rather than a woman's waist, it resembled a flower's stem.

Laura answered his gaze: "I don't feel well, Doctor."

"What's the matter? Careful!"

"It's my abdomen, Doctor. It feels heavy and it hurts so much that anyone else in my place would be in bed. This isn't the first time I've had this pain. It's been like this on other occasions, but I paid no heed. I didn't take care of myself and the ailment went away on its own, just as it began. I hope the same thing happens this time."

Dr. Barrios looked hard at her and sternly repeated the word "Careful!" adding: "Seek an examination without delay."

---

22   Translator's note: Mail was delivered rapidly via the Parisian system of pneumatic tubes.

***

Laura went pale for an instant, and a deathly cold chilled her blood; then she tried to compose herself, and as though casting out a horror, she strove to banish from her mind the notion of an internal illness.

Like a radiant sun she was proud of her body's beauty; would she lose it? Would she lose her delicate slenderness? Would she stop wearing corsets and the Louis XVI heels that lent her gait an undulating rhythm? If she truly was seriously ill, the news of her misfortune would greatly please the women who envied her success as a beautiful, elegant, and distinguished woman, celebrated in society.

Because of her beauty, grace, and habit of reclining on a sofa, as well as her virtue, her friends nicknamed her Madame de Récamier.[23]

***

Artfully frivolous and attractive like a doll, impassive, she devoted her entire existence to maintaining the prestige of being fashionable, her dresses dazzling in their exotic artistic taste. If at times she aroused passion, she responded with smiles and glances, and the moment a man began to flatter her insistently and she detected his passionate love, her spirit was overcome with such displeasure that she broke off their friendship completely, and fled the bothersome suitor, avoiding all contact.

She had become a widow at a very young age. Her married life was unhappy; she loved her husband with the sacred devotion of first love, but her husband's infidelity, and the long sleepless nights of delirious rage dissolving in tears, had submerged her in lethargic apathy.

This disillusionment suffered early in life shocked her young soul so violently that she found the world empty and impotent to kindle

---

23   Translator's note: Juliette Récamier was an early 19th-century Parisian salon hostess of legendary beauty whose name became synonymous with the type of sofa upon which she reclined. She was said to have never had sexual relations with her husband, who was rumored to be her biological father.

her heart's affective sensibilities. For six years she had been locked in battle, her will triumphing over any amorous instinct, effectively numbing her spirit. "My youth is dead," she declared triumphantly one day. "That is how I wanted it and that is how it shall be..." And from that time on, her life was a clear, sonorous whirlwind; at times the memory of the few years of happiness that had evaporated from her existence like clouds from the morning sky would elicit a sigh which she stifled, turning to the flattery of trivial flirtation and the deeply moving emotions of art.

Of all the arts, her favorite was painting, because it did not allow her to dream, to fashion hopes about the future, nor recall the monotony of bygone melancholy. The objective view fully beatified her, submerging her in oblivion like a saintly soul; in contrast, she avoided music like an old abandoned lover rekindling a destructive sentimentalism in which, nevertheless, the nostalgia of distant sorrows still throbbed.

Festive engagements and invitations filled her imagination such that, without feeling love, her life passed by in instinctive remembrances and candid timidity. A single passion dominated her, fascinated her blissfully. She loved her body as beauty is loved, and like a pagan she worshipped it; painstakingly she studied the aesthetic of movement, the flexibility of the line, and physical exercise, which she practiced daily under the direction of a skilled gymnast. Nevertheless, when a pair of lovers appeared before her eyes she would experience a sort of sentimental upheaval resembling an epileptic awakening, an internal shudder like a paralyzing winter, a tingling of the skin that lingered until suddenly it dominated her emotions. Her haughty character would speak arrogantly, and with the easy philosophy of an uncommon good humor, she would tell herself: "I possess unparalleled health, and this is the best lover, and the best life partner."

Chapter III

Dr. Barrios terrified her; if it was true that on several occasions the malaise had disappeared, it could also persist, which was inescapably alarming. Although she believed that her abstinent lifestyle protected her from any type of genital disease, she nevertheless recalled what she had heard Dr. Barrios say: "The origin of these ailments is rarely known."

Laura had felt unwell for a month when Dr. Barrios sounded the alarm.

Returning home after spending the day out visiting, she would often remark to her maid, "My friends live at such heights; whenever I go to take an elevator I see a sign that says: 'Temporarily closed for repairs.'"

***

When Laura left Mrs. D...'s house, where she had seen Dr. Barrios, a shadow of sorrow darkened her radiant eyes. At nightfall, profound anguish filled her with anxiety; she slept poorly, fitfully. The warning from Dr. Barrios was like a lightning bolt igniting a castle made of tinsel.

After long sleepless hours and several days of suffering, she began to feel a malaise so strong that she resolved to go to an ordinary gynecologist's office, even though her imagination rejected the obvious. Ashamed as though guilty of a crime, she dressed in a very simple ensemble, and under an assumed name, requested an appointment with a neighborhood doctor, fearful of being recognized if she went to one of the *en vogue* specialists she often encountered at the salons she frequented.

***

The diagnosis she heard could not have been more terrifying. "Madam," the doctor said, "if you are not serious about taking care of yourself, you'll have to undergo surgery within two years. Although you have not allowed me to perform an internal examination, your symptoms suggest that you may be seriously ill. Start by giving up high heels, stay off of your feet, and adhere momentarily to the hydrotherapy treatment I'm recommending in this prescription."

From that day on, the illness began to make itself known in earnest. Laura's attempts to to build up her hopes were futile; the force of the pain would awaken her to reality so cruelly that she could not contain her tears...she endured long, silent hours, and days and weeks of mute agony when her tears ran dry, until she regained strength from her own abandonment and solitude.

Desiring to hide her ailment from her Parisian social circle, she resolved to travel to Germany to continue treatment there, attracted in part by the fame of Prussian physicians. To this end, she took leave of her girlfriends, saying she would be traveling for pleasure.

The memory alone made her shiver as she waited for Dr. Castel in his Louis XVI parlor: what a cruel pilgrimage! More than a sufferer seeking health, she was a victim fleeing the knife. In vain she dressed modestly; whenever she went to a consultation with a leading light of German science, she took care not to wear any jewelry. Anyone unaware of her intentions would have supposed that she meant to penetrate the Whitechapel district of London or the *Apache* underworld of Paris. She thought that in simple dress she would be perceived as a person without wealth, and therefore, unable to pay the considerable sums charged for operations by surgeons at the pinnacle of their careers. She believed that by appearing poor, she would receive an impartial diagnosis, but all her precautions were futile: her aspect only betrayed her, for clearly, fortune is not easily hidden.

***

The first time she went to a famous German gynecologist was an affront to her exquisite feminine delicacy, accustomed to the indulgence and gallant extravagance of the French. At the home of the Berlin specialist, a female servant indicated that she was to remove her coat and hat before entering the parlor; Laura declined.

The spectacle that met her eyes in the waiting room was worthy of an Abel Faivre caricature.[24] If it had not merited tears, it would have provoked laughter: a row of women, some alone and others accompanied by their husbands, rested on sofas or chairs placed along the wall. The maid who had received them at the entrance had taken their hats, gloves, and coats one to two hours in advance. Thus uncovered, they displayed the corporeal deformity to which they were condemned by disease. In general, nearly all the women were stout and had bulging abdomens; some had a complexion resembling yellowish ceramic; their eyelids were stretched out and darkened by deep, sickly circles. A very thin, nearly emaciated woman caught Laura's eye, inspiring at once a vague mixture of equal parts pity and revulsion: her tremendously developed belly had skewed to the right side, protruding visibly. The ailing woman displayed her grotesque figure before the other patients, with no apparent shame. She was enduring her illness with admirable patience and resignation. She was the heroine of painful ugliness. Laura, who was beginning to understand this sort of illness, thought that she must have cancer in the most advanced stage of development. This caricaturesque exhibition, capricious work of human pain, sparked no outcry; oblivious to dissemblance, the women displayed themselves cartoonishly, without feeling feminine sorrow at beauty entombed in the pestilent grave of disease. In that room, the spirit of the German woman –devoid of flirtation, docile, yielding to the will of man– was on full display. A brunette of expired beauty was so obese that her hips and waist had grown wider than her shoulders, so that from her neck to her thighs she had become one deformed, perfectly straight mass of human

---

24   Translator's note: The French artist's early 20th-century satirical cartoons included
      caricatures of doctors and patients.

flesh. Her large black eyes, which surely had previously shone with
a glint of love, now appeared soulless, merely hinting at a flame extinguished by the scalpel. This brunette, whose beauty had been consumed by the clinic, was resigned to her circumstances like the other
ailing women.

The only person who was suffering, the only one who felt distressed, the only one who closed her eyes to shut out this portrait of
aesthetic depravity, was Laura; in turn, everyone present was staring
at her in astonishment. Only she had openly rebelled, keeping her
coat and hat in place; she was the woman who had disobeyed and
defied the physician's order for each patient to remove those garments
in the vestibule of the house. Of her ensemble, even her gloves remained intact, which earned her a look of profound displeasure from
Dr. Blumen when he instructed her to enter his office; surely he was
thinking of how much of his time she would waste by removing the
accessories that completed her toilette, while Laura mentally retorted:
"I am paying to receive a service."

***

Dr. Blumen is a prominent figure in Berlin; it is said that dukes
and princesses pass through his hands at birth. His appearance is cold,
grave, and circumspect, more austere than a trial judge. One who has
the fortune to be seen by Dr. Blumen must not ask him questions, but
only reply when spoken to... for is he not the king of gynecological
science?

Dr. Blumen sat at his desk, turned his back to Laura without ex-
cusing himself, and began to write, first telling her to undress while
gesturing toward a divan opposite him.

This time "undress" was meant literally, Laura understood, and
she proceeded to remove her hat, coat, etc., not without feeling deep
shame. Accursed fashion had replaced wide batiste drawers with
fitted silk knickers, which she was obliged to remove completely, and
this immodest action so embarrassed her that she blushed fiercely. She
scolded herself for not thinking of wearing, for this occasion, fuller
undergarments like a petticoat, which she could have left in place

even during the examination, concealing her legs in lace.

Fortunately for her, Dr. Blumen seemed to have forgotten that Laura was present, and she managed to remove her Saxon blue knickers, which matched her dress lining, of a darker blue, as well as her stockings and booties.

Hanging on the wall in front of her was a life-size painting of an operating table where a man lay with his entrails spilling out, red and bloody like a burst pomegranate; at his side was Dr. Blumen, brandishing a knife like a barber wields a razor blade.

Laura felt a chill when she saw the canvas, which immediately suggested the thought that she would be doomed to find herself in the same state as the figure in the painting.

From that moment on, gripped by indescribable terror and revulsion, she imagined Dr. Blumen not as an upstanding servant of humanity, but as a villain, a Jack the Ripper or something of the sort.

After a brief pause, making an effort to steady her voice, Laura dared to interrupt the doctor, who seemed to have completely forgotten her as he wrote and paged through various notebooks. "I'm ready," she said timidly.

He turned the chair where he was seated, and without getting up, addressed to her the following series of questions: "What is your name, madam? Where do you live? Street? Number?" Laura was taken aback, but unwilling to reveal her name, with feigned serenity, she answered all of the doctor's questions with falsehoods.

She found the questions so unrelated to her illness that for a moment, she felt as though she were answering a police officer. After fastidiously recording the information supplied, the doctor stood and walked over to her. His figure was arrogant, his appearance military; tall, solid, and ruddy, he resembled a cavalryman.

He gestured for Laura to lie down on the nearby divan, which she did with great difficulty, because her closely fitted skirt allowed only for deliberate movements that were no match for the circumstances.

Dr. Blumen's harsh physiognomy was no mystery to Laura, who sensed how displeased he was that she had taken more time than his other patients to prepare for the examination, and she was struck with deep emotion by the humiliating and indecorous position to which illness had subjected her.

Other than her husband, no man had approached her in this intimate manner, and her womanly modesty was offended; her Venus-like vanity was likewise wounded. Although she had never displayed her body unclothed, it had garnered the admiration of the most stylish artists and the praise of her admirers. Now, despite her beautiful nudity, she was being treated like disgusting rotten meat.

While all these ideas were forming and jumbling together in her mind, Dr. Blumen was squeezing and wringing her insides with his hands, blunt like a hammer and forceful like a press.

Suddenly, a sharp cry escaped the ailing woman's chest; it was not the sound emanating from a virgin's amorous anguish; the doctor's hand had found the illness, the site of the disease; there could be no doubt. His countenance contorted for an instant, then returned to his usual cold expression.

He left Laura's side and proceeded to wash his hands scrupulously.

I've disgusted him so!, Laura thought, overcome by pain, fear, and shame.

The via crucis of Laura's modesty was not yet complete. The doctor sat by her side and asked her to remove her blouse. Amid soft ruffles of Valencian lace and rainbow-colored ribbons, her breasts appeared like two blooming roses, splendid, firm, and perfumed.

The doctor took one, and it shrank back, trembling at the contact of his hand; then he tugged on the nipple so roughly that Laura let out a shriek, obliging the blushing doctor to apologize.

***

"What illness do I have?," Laura ventured to ask him before leaving, receiving a cold, harsh, distressing reply that did nothing to dispel her concern:

"You need surgery, madam."

The sky had grown dark; twilight muted by lace shades covering the large windows had fully penetrated the home, turning people and objects pallid. It was time to leave.

***

The words that Dr. Blumen had just uttered produced a great upheaval in Laura's spirit; a revolution of her entire being; a protest of her will against any good judgment or reasoning. As a woman accustomed to the dissemblance characteristic of higher social classes, she answered with a wry smile, after her ardent imagination rapidly devised a reply that would cause Dr. Blumen the greatest displeasure: "If it is essential that I have surgery, I will have to do it in Paris."

The blow could not have been more effective.

"Come to my clinic on Monday and you will hear my definitive diagnosis; I need to examine you twice." Saying this, the doctor stood and gestured, like a king, for her to leave. Laura could not contain a scowl; after leaving a twenty-mark piece on the desk and politely taking leave of the doctor, she hastily left the office just as concerned as when she arrived, if not more so.

***

Dr. Blumen's impression on her could not have been more lamentable; this most renowned, most aristocratic of Berlin's gynecologists would leave an ailing woman to the tremendous anguish occasioned by his words; he would have her endure two days without repose or solace, believing herself the prisoner of a terrible disease, rather than telling her immediately what he already knew and was reserving for later. These and other sad reflections preoccupied Laura while she slowly made her way down the city's wide, clean streets, where strange pedestrians at dusk resembled fugitive shades; finally, exhaustion compelled her to take an automobile back to the hotel, where she was alone with her sorrows.

Chapter IV

On a morning illuminated by a pale winter sun, Laura set off for Dr. Blumen's clinic, crossing an avenue in the Tiergarten, its Hohenzollern dynasty statues a procession of tombs.

Her heart heavy with pain, she crossed this sepulchral boulevard of stone excess, lightly tinged with autumnal greenery. Once inside Dr. Blumen's clinic, she was most struck by the heterogeneity of the patients, united only by their sex and disease. In a poorly furnished room, they awaited their turn. There was a screen in one corner behind which they were to remove their corsets, without any sort of comfort, not even a chair, or a mirror, or anything useful; it was a partially hidden corner, more appropriate for a man to remove or change his jacket; and it was there that a nurse directed Laura, holding her unfastened clothing so that it would not fall off, after she endured Dr. Blumen's second exam, which was similar to the first, except that the appearance of this clinic was repugnant; if completely antiseptic, it was nonetheless filthy to the eye.

The sheets were yellowish and coarse, and they were stained. Without emptying the vessels containing filth remaining from a treatment, they brought in the next patient, making no attempt to conceal this repulsive spectacle; likewise, water that had washed the putrefaction of a diseased body mixed with water from previous treatments, producing a nauseating sight. The linens covering the operating chair were not removed except in special cases, and they were still warm and wrinkled from the pressure of the previous set of buttocks when the next woman was to sit upon them.

***

Dr. Blumen's diagnosis completely reversed his first assessment.

"Madam, you have several small fibroids that make up a large growth; you do not need surgery."

Laura was stunned; two days ago, the same doctor had told her that she needed an operation, and now she was hearing the opposite. "At least, Doctor, is what I have malignant?"

"No, Madam."

"What about the pains I suffer?"

"It's nothing," said Dr. Blumen as he walked toward the door, opened it, and dismissed Laura, who as before had just left a 20-mark piece on a small table holding two enameled metal irrigators and a bottle of phenol that was leaking, despite being closed.

***

Two days later, Laura resolved to consult another physician, who, although not as famous as Dr. Blumen, enjoyed a reputation for great skill, which he clearly demonstrated. Less harsh than his colleague, he treated Laura courteously, and after asking her if there wasn't a family member accompanying her with whom he could discuss her illness, he apologized profusely for the grief he was about to cause her, and with that preamble, declared that her womb was full of "fibromiomas" requiring surgery; the expression on his face matched the situation: solemn, sorrowful, befitting a funeral mourner. He was thoroughly bewildered by how calmly Laura listened to him. She repeated what she had told Dr. Blumen –her upcoming return to Paris– and he echoed the request for a second exam at the clinic in order to give her a definitive diagnosis. There, he had no qualms about contradicting himself and declaring that she did not require an operation, just as his colleague had done before. To be fair, we must confess that he had a long conversation with Laura, and that he tried to convince her by every available means that she should remain in Berlin. Laura left with the firm intention to go to Paris, which she proceeded to do in such haste that she resembled a prison fugitive anxiously seeking cover.

***

Not long after arriving in Paris, she heard favorable remarks about Dr. Castel, who was of Oriental origin but Parisian education. The recommendation could not have been more positive: "He's a very talented doctor," she was told, which was enough to convince her in advance to submit to whatever Dr. Castel told her. Nevertheless, uncertainty overwhelmed her soul, and she was deeply saddened by the cynicism that the German physicians had instilled in her spirit. "This is the last doctor I will consult," she told herself as she waited for Dr. Castel to arrive. The painful disappointment she had already experienced had so disillusioned her that she had neither the desire nor the strength to continue making inquiries that resulted only in heightening her fears.

Chapter V

Dr. Castel's Louis XV sitting room was full of patients, women who, if not elegant, were at least correctly dressed and whose appearance scarcely betrayed the slightest hint of illness.

A male servant led Laura to the physician's office, where he received her with great deference, like a gentleman at a soiree. The room was spacious and drenched in midday light, like a painter's studio. The far wall was made of windows that filled the room with luminous brilliance. A beautiful fire in a large marble hearth lent the warmth of a greenhouse.

The doctor invited his new client to sit on a crimson velvet sofa, and he sat opposite her on the end of a snow-white divan covered in impeccable oilcloth. Dr. Castel's Carmelite-brown eyes fixed upon Laura's, and he was moved by her distressed, pleading gaze. A wave of sympathy passed undetected through the two spirits, one yearning, the other inquisitive.

***

Dr. Castel went to the next room, opening a large glass door. Silently, meticulously, after donning a white linen coat, he began to fill a large clear glass basin with water to wash his hands and disinfect a speculum...

This room was just as spacious as the one before, but its light was even more powerful; all the walls were painted white and lined with tall glass shelves supported by nickel-plated bars. A large case entirely of glass held the surgical instruments, perfectly clean and gleaming like precious metals in a jeweler's display. Everything appeared immaculately pure, without a speck of dust or the slightest stain, like a house of snow. The treatment table had been placed in the center like a throne, elevated and bathed in intense light.

The timbre of the doctor's voice was sweet and the accent of his words was warm, infusing Laura's soul with tranquility like quiet waters. Gallantly, he took Laura by the hand and invited her up onto the auscultation table, first telling her that she could remove her dress so as not to wrinkle it, which she was very pleased to do, protecting the pleats the tailor had so skillfully fashioned in the skirt.

Dr. Castel helped her to lie down; his attitude reflected a maternal sense of compassion. She was pale, a secret anguish weighing heavy on her chest; he was pensive; both remained silent. Laura reclined comfortably; the doctor put a cushion under her head, then placed her feet in the stirrups that were raised at the end of the bed...

The doctor's steps resounded with a strident echo in the stillness of the room; the moment was solemn. A vague, sinister portent flooded the clinic with melancholy.

The immensity of her sorrow drew her thoughts to the unfathomable, the infinite, the hideousness of diseased matter, and mixed with all this was a sense of wounded modesty, so shameful to Laura that her exposed legs, unusually white under the piercing examination room light, trembled like languishing branches.

The doctor wasn't looking at her; his eyes were fixed on the instruments before him, and his placid brow seemed to reveal a halo of thought oblivious to all his surroundings except the warmed, oiled speculum he was slowly, gently inserting into Laura's body.

"I won't feel any pain?," she asked fearfully.

"None, madam, I promise, do not worry," the doctor replied, looking at her as though shaken from a deep sleep.

When he had finished the visual examination, the doctor proceeded to the manual examination, which he endeavored to perform with the fine delicacy of the most selfless lover. He positioned himself by Laura's side, and without looking at her, his eyes downcast, he slid his hands gently, one inside and the other outside of her pelvis. Warm and strong, his hands were infused with the sensuousness of a caress rather than the coldness of a surgeon. Laura forgot the physician for a moment, absorbed in the attentive, solemn man before her. She felt blood rushing through her veins; a fever flooded her body, pearls of water beaded her forehead. The doctor drew closer to the head of the bed, looking at her tenderly; after saying, "Forgive me, madam, one moment and I will be finished," he began to softly press her breasts with delicate sensitivity uncommon in an examination. A light carmine tinged Laura's cheeks, and she did not manage a reply; breathlessness betrayed her unrequited amorous anguish.

Ardent and throbbing with emotion, her flesh exuded a warm, intoxicating musky perfume. She was covered only by linen and Valencian lace, its white monotony broken by rosy flowers and ribbons.

Quite in spite of himself, the doctor was distracted from his medical task, intoxicated by the woman's feminine charm; he could not disregard the sight of a young woman so beautiful that she looked less like a patient than an offering of the Gods upon a bed of love. Then he continued the pelvic examination, which he had momentarily interrupted. Something more powerful than any dream or chimera commanded his soul: the imperious power of his passion for science. The fine touch of his fingers, accustomed to detecting maladies of the internal organs, soon found the sensitive area. The doctor's physiognomy contorted and the sense of absence from all his material surroundings appeared in his eyes once more.

A plaintive sigh escaped Laura's lips.

"Is the pain here?" the doctor asked, placing both hands at the site of the disease.

"Yes," Laura replied, "the pain there is sharp, piercing..."

Even greater was the pain of her soul, convinced that she was ill.

As in childhood she felt fragile, wishing her mother were there to embrace her, put her arms around her and sob profusely, drench her in tears, until she had freed herself from her anguish. Like a little girl, she felt a pressing need to be cared for, to receive a caress denoting shelter and protection, a touch that would speak more clearly than words, telling her that suffering is alleviated when love is by the patient's side...

But she heard no consolation, only the sorrowful, hidden torment of her being, overflowing wildly and ready to burst.

An imposing silence dominated the room as the doctor said: "Do not be alarmed, madam; please forgive me if I cause you any pain; just one moment, to gain certainty, and I will trouble you no longer."

***

What good has my youth of chastity and deprivation done me, my life perhaps soon to be extinguished without the pleasure of love?, thought Laura as the doctor, ever gallant, helped her down from the table, his strong arm around her waist. Laura's eyes seemed to devour those of the doctor, while his revealed nothing; the typical enigmatic mask of all doctors made his thoughts impenetrable.

As she left, Laura promised to follow the prescribed treatment.

They agreed that she must come to the clinic three times per week, and after hearing his reassurance that she would soon be completely well, all the sorrows that had been tormenting her vanished from her soul with the naivete of a little girl. From that day on, her greatest concerns were replacing her corset with an elastic one without whalebones, and ordering an empire-waist dress that she believed would suit her better than her others with the new corset.

Chapter VI

Dr. Castel was born in Constantinople. Turks and Armenians were among his forebears. In one of the horrible slaughters suffered by the Armenians, nearly all of his relatives perished, and his parents, who had previously enjoyed a large fortune, were left destitute. A wealthy uncle who took care of Dr. Castel in his childhood was the only one who managed to save his fortune from the catastrophe; as there were orphans and widows in the family at the time of the uncle's death, Dr. Castel, who in his youth anticipated that inheritance, was obliged to give it up for the benefit of those less fortunate relatives.

He relied on his profession and the brave fortitude of his spirit to stay on his feet in the battle of existence. At a tender age, he entered into marriage with a distinguished young lady, to whom he was bound only by slight affection, which failed to become a stronger feeling that could become love as he had expected, but, on the contrary, quickly dissipated amid the bourgeois dealings of conjugal life. Dr. Castel entered marriage without lofty expectations, knowing that in order to work in the gynecology profession, it was necessary to acquire the respectability that the condition of marriage confers in society; moreover, he wanted to have a home and all the material comforts that go with it, to free himself from dealing with the details of everyday existence; he found this essential, desirous as he was to devote himself entirely to his profession, without diverting precious time to trifles. One day he was introduced to an eligible lady, and as the young woman was kind and the doctor had no inclination for the playboy lifestyle, he thought it would be most practical to accept the first woman presented to him, thus managing, at least, to stabilize his life just as he had projected.

The marital union did not last long; the young woman's frivolity distanced her intellectually from her husband, and with that moral remoteness, physical detachment soon followed.

Keen to preserve the spiritual tranquility that was so necessary in the practice of his profession, Dr. Castel was able to establish a fraternal friendship acceptable to them both. Two children helped to maintain the appearance of a happy home: a girl who was studious and thoughtful like her father, and a boy who was banal and shallow like his mother.

Dr. Castel's profession was his passion, like an ancient poet's muses; science represented for him what art means to the artist.

Imperious and energetic, he did not entrust his work to any nurse, but personally ensured the full asepsis of his clinic as well as its meticulous cleaning.

Before he could establish himself and gain a large clientele, he had to develop skills of uncommon focus and talent.

The struggle of existence and the noble ambition to make a name for himself were the passions that dominated him. His spirit, his Oriental imagination, his abundantly tender nature, were steeped in the hazy, provocative atmosphere of Paris like a caterpillar in a cocoon. His amorous temperament had developed unseen, stunted like a plant hidden away in the sheltered greenhouse of clinics and hospitals, never finding the reach of a benevolent palm tree or a tranquil oasis to interrupt the parched desert in which his passionate temperament withered; nevertheless, what predominated in him, above all ambition or instinct, was serene reason achieved through work and logic, through the inescapable tribulations of supporting his family and the even greater emotional burden of his patients' health. He had spent his early youth indifferent to the turbulent exuberance of the student, and his being had never been shaken by love, and yet, it can be said that without knowing it, his capacity for passion united the power of his exquisite intelligence with an ardent temperament.

***

When Dr. Castel received Laura's visit, he was experiencing a time of moral weariness, of amorous apathy. He was forty years old, but he appeared older still. He had been aged by a life of incessant labor, sleepless nights, and emotion. In truth, what most afflicted and consumed his nature was the nervous excitation that came over his organism when a seriously ill patient was in his care; fortunately, the spectacle of death rarely injured his sensitive spirit, and those entrusted to his care generally recovered from their ailments, preserving the memory of Dr. Castel with the placid joy of health.

***

Laura's case worried him that winter afternoon as snow lined the houses, saddening the city with bleak whiteness. From the windows of his clinic, the Siberian landscape so distressed him that his thoughts turned with melancholy to the bright and colorful Bosphorus, whose shores had been his cradle. Nostalgia for the sun flooded his soul...

The servant soon arrived and switched on the electricity. Outside, night was falling over the sad city like a white pall of annihilation over a wilderness. Dr. Castel left the clinic and headed home in silence, his feet sliding cautiously over the snow crystallizing the avenues.

The figure of Laura had not left his imagination. Who was this beautiful young woman, chaste despite her tempting and sensuous aspect? But this thought crossed his mind fleetingly like a wingbeat. The disease was the idea that dominated his brain. Like a fighter of the intangible, he saw that a new enemy had just presented itself concealed within the body of a goddess: the health of Laura. He had no doubt that her condition was poor, that she required meticulous care and great devotion; no less delicate was the state of her soul.

"It's fortunate that she's come to me," he told himself as he mechanically sidestepped the snow crunching under his footsteps like crushed insects.

The patient's eyes, so infinitely sad and dreamy, her melancholy tone, and her refined, spiritual conversation had made a sweet, agreeable impression on Dr. Castel. He took pleasure in remembering her as a tender apparition that lulled him like the music of a secret, vibrant hymn in the austere ambiance with which his profession tormented him.

Chapter VII

Laura's second visit shook him. His apathy awoke with visible emotion; in vain he strove to appear indifferent, to rely on the studied mask under which all physicians hide their feelings. His expressive, mobile physiognomy revealed the turbulence of his soul; in his eyes, in his gestures, in his exaggerated solicitousness, Laura observed that in addition to the doctor, she was also in the presence of a man who was yearning to please her and anxious to prevent her suffering; moreover, exquisite sensitivity allowed her to comprehend, instinctively, that the doctor was a man of good taste, capable of appreciating the beauty of her shape, the splendid lines and delicate contours with which God had favored her body, which so flattered her vanity that she forgot her illness during the mortifying treatments she underwent.

Her flesh, exposed to the gaze of Dr. Castel, quivered at the touch of his hands. Saddened by modesty, she was delirious for a cavern of infinite blackness to eternally entomb her nudity...

Making a great effort to appear serene so that the doctor would not observe the carmine flush of her cheeks, with the warmth of a flame rising up from her chest, she would tell herself, "I hope I'll grow accustomed to the nudity the clinic requires of me," but as soon as she found herself outside, she would imagine that the doctor's eyes were following her with that strange fixity that seemed to offer her in love a remote enigma of extinct generations, revealing forgotten sensuousness—an unknown love able to revive the traditions of ancestral lovers, of consuming passion, maddening joy, stupefying oblivion, and lethal abandonment.

Dominated by this idea as she left the clinic, she sometimes forgot that she was dressed, and the physical sensation of nudity that she had experienced persisted with such a sensation of cold that she had to touch her clothing, fearful that she had left it unfastened and a breeze had penetrated to her skin. Upon returning to reality, she flushed deeply with embarrassment, fearful that some passerby had seen her. Other times, at the front door, she would look around to make sure no one was looking, like a married woman leaving her lover's house, and hurry into the first car she found.

***

Before long, a friendship grew between doctor and patient: intimate and fraternal initially, amorous later.

Unaccustomed as the doctor was to moments of peace, Laura's visits provided him the joy of an oasis in the midst of the pained caravan that came to him thirsting for health. He arranged the appointments of his other patients in such a way that he could devote a full hour to her, during which they dedicated ample time to the jocularly instructive conversation they longed for, enjoyed only by those who have a beatific spirit and light in mind.

***

Laura began to feel relief after receiving a few treatments, and her nerves stabilized and she returned to her customary good humor.

She did not notice the passing of time as a few weeks slipped by, thanks to the doctor's seductive appeal, his delicate and refined manners, and the selflessness and professional delicacy he lavished upon her.

Drawn to the charm of the doctor's companionship, Laura gave up her social relationships without noticing or missing them, obliged by her illness, whose treatment required absolute rest.

One day on the way to his office, she passed a florist shop and bought a beautiful bouquet of fragrant violets; it was Carnival time; the memory of the parties she had attended the year before and the thought that she could not enjoy her usual diversions saddened her demeanor.

Paris was vibrating in unison in a single festive peal of laughter. Carefree young ladies laughed with the mischievous merriment of a street dance; pedestrians laughed, caught up in the wave of the masquerade; grand ladies laughed from the depths of carriages fleeing the dazzling color of the popular clown parade; old people laughed, forgetting age and the open grave where death beckons with each passing step; the streets, avenues, and boulevards laughed too, peppered with confetti and festooned with streamers.

The sweaty, panting mobs parted in a final mobile celebration, turbulent and bewildering.

Laughter echoed, blending with the whisper of amorous dialogues, easy conquests, pressing engagements. Couples held one another in loving embrace and the murmur of kisses lacked fantasy in the wanton hubbub of the public street. Laughter on the day of Carnival tolerated all, celebrated all—laughter of sin, laughter of love, of spontaneous, carefree joy.

The sky was tinged with a tenuous burgundy gleaming over a somber blue. A rare light was holding back the dusk, protecting the popular festivities.

Laura fled the hubbub, pensive, seeking recent memories of happiness.

With vivid intensity, she imagined the parties she had attended the year before, and she was saddened to be unable to enjoy her customary diversions at present. A faint shadow of melancholy appeared on her face.

Greeting the doctor, she said, "I came across these violets on the way here, doctor, and I thought of you."

The doctor grew pale with emotion, and lacking words to thank Laura for her attention, effusively, he bowed gallantly and kissed both her hands; but he was so moved that when he spoke, like a boy, he found only the words he least desired: "Thank you very much, madam. Words cannot express my appreciation for this gift. I'll take them to my wife this evening."

Laura smiled, and the shadow of sorrow in her eyes darkened.

Chapter VIII

As Laura entered the doctor's office, he hurried over to her and said: "Don't remove your coat, madam, come with me and see your violets; I've put them in my window, so the heat from the fireplace doesn't wilt them. I thought that you brought them for me, and I didn't want to be apart from them. During free moments in between patients, I lean out and breathe this perfume, thinking of you."

Speaking these words, he held Laura's hands in his own, which she permitted with fraternal ease.

"Thank you, doctor. Yes, it's true that I brought them for you. I can't deny it," Laura replied. She blushed, her heart swelling with pleasure.

"I'm sad, doctor; I'm bored," she went on, trying to change the subject.

"Why?"

"I can't go for walks, I can't get dressed, my body has become deformed, I've lost my figure without my corset, none of my dresses fit well. I'm going to lose the shape of my waist; I fear that even when I'm cured it won't be like before."

"Complaining about your body!" the doctor interrupted, adding: "Few women have a body more beautiful than yours, madam. Do you imagine that thinness holds any appeal? A body without the roundness of breasts or the tender curve of hips doesn't look womanly."

Laura listened to him with pleasure, but as the doctor was not a worldly man, and was unaccustomed to salon flattery, he feared he had said too much, and broke the spell of the exchange, adding: "All the Spanish women who have come to my clinic are like you, madam:

they have lovely figures. Yesterday I wished I was a painter. I saw a woman who appeared unremarkable in modest dress, but nude she is the most beautiful Venus on the face of the earth; her skin glows like mother-of-pearl; her breasts are firm and her nipples are pink like new flower buds. I should have liked to kneel before that body and kiss it devotedly, like a believer kissing the Virgin's mantle."

Laura felt a secret resentment germinating in her chest, and she replied scornfully: "A doctor should never see the woman—only the patient."

Meanwhile, she was fumbling hastily with the ribbons of her clothing and the fastenings of her dress, which were growing increasingly tangled, approaching disaster. The doctor hurried to her side and slowly began to undress her, with the great devotion of a groom on his wedding night, sensitive to his bride's virginal blush: first the skirt, then the blouse, the corset, and garter straps.

"Clearly you have practiced this, doctor," Laura said, still testy, not appreciating the doctor's submissiveness.

Seated in a chair, the doctor continued his work without replying. He had Laura standing before him, and she left him to his task, because every time she intervened she only managed to tear some lace or pull a tie the wrong way.

"Allow me, madam," he'd say. "Please relax."

"I forgot to put on a petticoat today; since it's not in fashion, I only wear one when I come here."

"No matter, the chemise will do, and it won't be the first time; do you remember the first day I saw you? I don't count, I'm not a man. All I want is for you to be comfortable."

Lightly veiled in transparent linen, Laura was superbly beautiful...

The doctor's manner was so devoted and affectionate that Laura finally relaxed, and it dawned on her that, far from not being a man, as he had just said, the doctor had a very distinguished figure, a quite charming voice, and a special appeal that was rare in men: selflessness.

A profound, sincere, intimate friendship had grown between them due to the frequency of their visits, the harmony of their ideas, the delightful conversations they enjoyed together, and also to the contact and modesty to which illness subjected her.

Laura's honesty and excessive initial timidity had transformed into a carefree familiarity that no longer unsettled her, although it did make her cheeks glow.

The doctor realized the displeasure his words had caused her; it was not difficult to comprehend that the lovely woman's vanity could not tolerate mention of another beauty in her presence, and remorseful like the best penitent, he felt inclined to ask for her forgiveness...

***

Once Laura had lain down on the small bed where the treatments were performed, the doctor came over to her and said with a smile before beginning his work, "The impression a woman makes through physical attraction alone is worth very little; for me, its effect is secondary. The most beautiful women have the least talent and soul; the banality of their thoughts generally makes them unbearable. Think about my profession, Laura; think of the countless beautiful and ugly women who have passed through my clinic over my long career: some are sensual, some voluptuous, others cold, unfeeling. Think for a moment, madam, of the confidences, the confessions I hear every day; I see not just women's bodies, but also their souls; this is my whole life, never finding a single being with the talent and flair to break through that banality, never seeing eyes that speak not in trifles, but in the language of intelligence—that intellectual mystification that says more than any voluptuous sensation."

The doctor had drawn so near that Laura could feel his warm breath caressing her chest; a quickening of her skin paralyzed her, and her insides were seized in yearning torment. The doctor was looking at her, and his ardent eyes were like a consuming flame, like a hot, parched desert. Feigning serenity, but still mordant, Laura replied: "What you say is striking, doctor; I know many women who are both attractive and talented..."

"No, no," the doctor hastily replied, "you have not observed them well. The ones with uncommon talent do not know feminine charm and sweetness, and soon display a virile temperament. I'm certain that what all men prefer to praise most in you is your beauty; nevertheless, what I admire most in you, aside from your sweet and delicate charm, is the clarity of your intelligence, your quick comprehension, your beautiful reason, combined with such feminine flair."

Laura laughed candidly, with the freedom of a bird crossing the sky, and extending a fine white arm adorned with several gemstone bracelets, she commanded: "Enough talk –time to work."

One of her breasts escaped the neckline of the chemise; the doctor took it in his hands and pressed it softly with his fingers. "The glands aren't irritated," he said. "You must be much relieved."

A few moments later, inserting the speculum, he seemed troubled for a moment, but quickly composed himself and continued placidly: "You are extremely congested; for the sake of your health, madam, with the temptations at hand every day, do not do something reckless that would prove fatal. Listen to me: as a doctor, I know where the imperious demands of nature can lead any woman, in spite of any sense of honor and no matter how chaste she may be. I beg you not to be offended, Laura. Do not believe that I doubt you; I'm speaking to you this way to fulfill my duty. The physician is the one talking. At this moment I'm not your friend."

A stifled sigh escaped Laura's lips; she opened her heavy eyes wide; with effort, she seemed to awaken from somnolence and to regain her senses, turning away from a pleasurable dream. The dignity of her spirit, burdened by matter, spoke at last.

"No, doctor, don't worry. A woman always has reserves unknown to men that are greater than any desire. As long as my heart is not moved, I'm always certain to triumph."

As she said this, her body throbbed like a fish seeking water, and a secret inner voice was saying deep within her body: "Take me in your arms, hold me, our bodies uniting so that I feel your soul join in amorous union..."

"I'm tired, doctor, I feel discouraged, I don't want this torment to go on any longer. When will I be cured?" And her lips continued to race, as if words were a way to run from her desires, from the inevitable, perhaps. "What a demoralizing illness, putting me in this condition, detesting sensuality as I do! Give me a remedy, doctor, I don't want to go on this way any longer."

"There is nothing, Laura, absolutely nothing. Two more treatments and you will have your freedom. I know what you'll say: 'I've always had it, and I've never used it.' But what you don't know is that the demands of reproduction speak more loudly in women than in men. I greatly fear, Laura, that when you leave this clinic, you will accept a lover, and God knows what that will do to your condition. I'm saying this only out of the great interest you inspire in me, madam, just as I would do for my wife."

These last words produced in Laura the effect of the medicine she desired, breaking the sensuous enchantment.

Chapter IX

"Tomorrow is a holiday," Dr. Castel said, like a schoolboy antic-ipating a day of revelry. "If you like, Laura, we'll go to eat on the banks of the Seine."

They took the little steamer full of passengers that skimmed over the river, cloudy and channeled like a foul gutter.

Like a modest bourgeois couple, they mixed with young female workers and their lovers, happily enjoying their hours free from the week's labor.

They had such flair, they expressed such joy in their powdered faces brightened with rouge, that Laura could not but admire those beings strengthened by work and by love.

In a small restaurant, Laura and the doctor sat at a small table in a corner. He said, "What most entertains me when I am in public is observation. This society is unfamiliar to you; look at that girl, the one in the toque—she's a third wheel. Do you see her getting up and looking around at the other tables? Clearly, she's looking for someone to invite her to eat. Perhaps she doesn't even have enough to pay for the steamer back to Paris."

"This is sad, very sad," Laura replied. "The life of women who sell caresses is tolerable when cloaked in luxury; love needs golden carriages and garlands of roses. When it comes with poverty it's a sickly sight; it pains me infinitely."

The girl in the toque soon returned to her place, looking satisfied and happy on the arm of an official who had been a stranger to her moments earlier. "Oh! The psychology of these souls—I would like to know it!" Laura exclaimed.

"It's not difficult, my friend: no soul exists in these beings, only poverty or vice."

***

The last steamer of the evening slipped away right before the oblivious pair, caught up in the light conversation of a romantic Sunday stroll.

Laura looked alarmed, believing there was no means of transportation to return home; but the doctor reassured her: "I know all of these suburbs, madam. Don't worry, we're one kilometer from the station where we can catch a train. The moon will light our way. Besides, the walk along the river isn't strenuous. Take my arm."

The melancholy of the moon seemed to have influenced their spirits: they spoke of sad things; he told her about his life as a student, his struggles and how every day he would travel these very streets on his way to the academy of medicine, and she told him of her childhood, of her parents' city, of past civilizations, oppressed peoples, the decadent Arabs whose millenary artistic temperament she so admired, and of her paralyzed mother who used to tell her legends of Abencerrages and sultanas.

***

The moon went dark behind mournful veils of passing black clouds. As they walked along the riverbank, the water of the Seine glinted with the far-off lights of restaurants, like a reminiscence of the distant boulevards' luminous festivity.

The doctor was constantly concerned about Laura; he persistently asked if she was tired, and when she took any misstep, he held her by the waist. When the breeze picked up, he wrapped her shawl around her just as a mother would do for her daughter. Laura was deeply grateful for such attentiveness, holding his hands in wordless reply.

***

The doctor was the first to speak after walking a few meters in silence, as though continuing an ongoing conversation from a moment earlier.

"In all honesty, Laura, my work as a surgeon is complete. If you ever feel the slightest discomfort in the future, you need only return."

Laura hadn't thought that inevitably her treatment would end and the time would come to say goodbye. It seemed to her that the doctor was moving up her release because he wasn't interested in seeing her, and for a moment she felt some offense; nonetheless, she overcame her shock, easily comprehending that the doctor was right, that inevitably this day of separation had to come.

Chapter X

Laura spent a week attending parties and outings, losing herself in her former life of diversion, making up for lost time, as she would say, but nostalgia for the clinic always came over her, and she was obsessed with the memory of Dr. Castel, sometimes attentive like a suitor and avoiding her at other times when she thought he was most overcome; at times she wanted to conquer his love; it flattered the vanity of her beauty to capture the love of the man who saw in her the only physical ailment capable of staunching all desire.

"This is a formidable ambition," she told herself; nonetheless, she was comforted by the idea that Dr. Castel would surely be no Ramón Llull, as well as the thought that she was not in such a lamentable state as his heroine.[25]

No outer sign of ugliness revealed the ailment located deep within her body; it was profound and hidden like her sorrow.

How she enjoyed a respite from lamentation in the seclusion of her bedroom, where alone and pensive she still looked young and beautiful, not a single trace of the foul disease marking her warm, milky flesh! With the devotion of a saint, sheltered by the silence of night, she relived her childhood in the convent, visions of female saints who martyrized their bodies, tormenting themselves with cilices and burns, still not comprehending such sublime renunciation; and she plunged into the haze of torture, not discerning the diaphanous halo of ethereal holy women repulsed by the body; moaning at the yearning convent and her present passion for tangible form, she

---

25 Translator's note: The medieval philosopher, one of the first to write in the Catalán vernacular, was said to have given up his hedonistic lifestyle after a woman he desired revealed her cancerous breasts.

sighed over such sickly aberrations of pure souls, their predestined divine gifts invisible to her.

Chapter XI

Fifteen days of separation passed, during which Laura's desire to see the doctor again was irresistible, and for that reason, she didn't dare do it, until one afternoon her abdominal discomfort forced her to go to the doctor, who couldn't hide the happy expression that crossed his face when he saw her.

Laura appeared before him with a new look; she had gone back to using her corset as before; her body had been perfected and she looked elegant, coquettish, and youthful, like springtime coloring the city with the light of life.

In appearance, Laura's illness was of no importance; a few ichthyol treatments would be sufficient to relieve the inflammation that was troubling her.

***

Dr. Castel was the sort of man who was not seductive in love; preoccupied and absorbed in his science, he allowed them to come to him. Laura inspired in him an affection so great that he couldn't manage to define it; he felt attracted to her with irresistible force; nevertheless, he contained the instinctive impulse propelling him toward her, because Laura's ailment frightened him. Like an icy phantom, her illness paralyzed his sentiments. To what state would amorous relations bring her? What would be the condition of her pathology upon awakening her senses in the critical stage it was entering?

With her flirtatious charm and faith in her beauty, Laura believed like a pagan that the latter would triumph over any reflection, fear, or displeasure that could be inspired by the reproductive ailment she suffered; she had hope in the formidable triumph of sensual power over humanity, and she believed it capable of conquering even diseased matter. Emboldened by this idea, she became the serpent's Eve. Like the mother of paradise, she did not find it difficult to seduce the man.

The doctor loved Laura, but as his life had always been directed by the force of inevitable events, he was accustomed to disciplining his will, such that, without great effort, he opted to play the role of the resigned man assigned to him by fate.

Born in the city of perfumed carnations, of the oppressive, blazing sun, where children play castanets with a distant, monotonous echo like a lament of slaves and a clanking of chains, Laura felt herself dying with the impassioned force of her ancestral lineage; although she was descended from a noble family, she had long ago lost the right to this aristocratic legacy. During one of the infinite hours of immobility to which she was condemned by paralysis, her mother had told her that one of her grandmothers, madly in love, had defied her father's wishes by marrying a young Arab of noble descent. The family nevertheless considered her dishonored by a union mixing Castilian and Moorish blood. Such a disgrace to her lineage earned her the alienation of her family. Blinded by love, the Spanish woman preferred to follow her lover, relocating with him to Africa, leaving her country and her parents behind. A few years after separating from her family, she returned to Cádiz, where her first and only daughter was born, a stunning beauty. Shortly after the daughter's birth, the husband died, and the widow remained in Spain, where her daughter married a rich local merchant.

Years later, Laura was born, a belated fruit of this union in the twilight of youth. When she was only eight years old, her parents decided to move to Paris, where they died when she was still very young. Relatives on her father's side took care of the girl until, much to their chagrin, she married a young artist who had little respect for the religious traditions of Spanish households.

Laura was educated in a convent by nuns who, at her family's request, strove to develop piety and fervor in her heart; given the girl's exuberant temperament and the imaginative force of her nature, her teachers' efforts transformed her as she reached womanhood into a mystic of art. Her knowledge of painting was surprising; she had toured the most important museums in the world, and her opinions were heard with the attention paid to the best critic. Her art library was considered one of the most complete among aficionados, and if she herself had not learned to paint, it was due to her insuperable in- dolence when it came to any sort of effort. She had an extraordinary ease of comprehension and could perform profound analyses like a psychologist, but she was not capable of producing.

Chapter XII

The rooms were suffused with a suffocating atmosphere in the first heat of summer. The doctor had raised the large jalousie windows and opened the windows in the treatment room, providing a view of the lush, tender greenery of the adjoining garden, which belonged to an orphanage run by nuns.

Before Laura shed her clothing, as she was obliged to do whenever she went to the clinic, the doctor carefully closed the windows, accentuating the perfume of oak and foliage that had penetrated rooms where not a single atom of air circulated. Laura and the doctor alike felt the exuberant, unconscious joy instilled in tropical temperaments by the lusty nature of summer. They felt the joy of young innocence, speaking childishly and laughing like kids for no reason or cause whatsoever.

Laura was standing with her body hidden behind the treatment bed where she rested her arms as though it were a box seat railing. She was waiting for the doctor to finish preparing his instruments, which was taking much longer than usual. He approached Laura slowly, put one arm around her back, and brushed her cheek, saying, "Give me a kiss, Laura."

Paralyzed, she had no time to reply except to instinctively return the slow, intense, loving kiss the doctor pressed upon her lips. For a second, her spirit reacted and she attempted to break away from the doctor, but it was futile, because his touch was cauterizing her with burning force. The doctor did not seem to notice this ephemeral reaction, and he devoured her with insatiable, tender kisses...

Then they looked at one another and neither one seemed surprised, nor did they make any mention of the manifestation of love they had just lavished upon one another, as it felt so natural for what they had so long hidden in their hearts to overflow.

"Do you feel better, madam?" the doctor asked, kissing her hands before leaving her side.

"Yes," Laura replied, sighing deeply.

"I feel well too, I feel so well!" he exclaimed effusively, helping her up to the treatment bed.

Once reclining, she was overcome by an irresistible sensation of lushness, and she covered her face with both hands and said: "I can't do this anymore."

The doctor hurried to her side and asked her to get up.

He nearly carried her to the other operating room, more intimate than the first. Laura reclined on a white lacquered divan that resembled a little girl's bed in its elegance and diminutive proportions. She was just as white; her face gleamed like ivory and her black eyes were lucid, aflame with love. The doctor left her alone for a moment, returning with a glass of cold water for her to sip.

"You are in such a state, Laura," he said, sitting by her side, "that it will be impossible to perform any treatment, although God knows you need it... Let's not do anything rash; my duty as a doctor comes before everything else; you have trusted me with your health, and I am responsible for it."

Laura never expected to hear such words at this moment bereft of reason, when her being was vibrating, trembling, her body and soul stunned, ready to be consumed in a fiery abyss.

Like dead vanity resurrected, her pride spoke; the beautiful woman, the scorned female, was hurt. Perhaps the doctor felt repulsed by her ailing body; the disease was more powerful than any desire or sensuousness, and it was driving him away from her, from the enamored Venus. At that instant she had no doubt, she felt convinced that she had inspired in him only spiritual affection, and she sadly recalled that during the moment of supreme love when a kiss bloomed on her lips, although his arms embraced her, their bodies had not the slightest contact; was that vitality, that exuberant health, instinctively rejecting the proximity of her pale flesh, poor in sanguine coloration?

On other occasions when she was healthy, thirsting for romance, Laura had longed to feel passion reminding her of the bliss of first love; at that moment, far from being crestfallen, the blow to her perceived sovereignty stirred all her beliefs, her prejudices, her fears, in a mute protest of tormented yearning. As though propelled by a strange force, she began to speak with uncharacteristic verbosity.

"Why don't you tell me you love me, doctor? Please, I want to know if you love me."

Seated on the edge of the divan, the doctor put his strong arm around her waist and pulled her close. He smiled at her affectionately. The resignation of an Arab traveler walking into the immense desert appeared in his eyes with a reflection of his soul.

Laura took his hands, kissing them with passion, and exclaimed, "These hands are so good to me."

"This love is yours, Laura, make no mistake; I inspire only gratitude in you."

With a rapid movement, Laura sat upon the doctor's knees, and endeavoring to erase the painful impression his words had produced, devoured him in effusive kisses, mad with joy... The doctor forgot that he was a physician, that he was with a nervous woman who was excited by illness, and he forgot, too, that he was in his office, where a considerable number of patients had been waiting for his attention for over an hour, and he made the white divan into a bed of caresses...

The enjoyment was intense, extraordinary, like never before: intelligence, soul, and senses united in pleasure. During the reality of love, Laura's attitude was one of selflessness. A line of white glass vessels containing topaz liquid for analysis by the doctor were positioned right in front of her, and she could not look away from the patients' secretions. This sight prevented her from focusing her senses and feeling the supreme spasm.

Chapter XIII

Returning to reason after the pleasure of love often includes some anxious moments. Like a pair of criminals trying to cover up traces of a crime, they silently scrambled to prepare the treatment equipment and put everything in order.

Once she was dressed, Laura opened up the window overlooking the adjacent convent garden: orange light colored the blooming acacias; the amaranthine glow, warm and luminous, reached her chest, drawing her gaze upward; she lifted her bowed head and saw the setting sun, large and majestic in its final gleam.

***

"Laura, how do you feel? Have I caused you any harm?" the doctor inquired tenderly.

"No," she answered without looking at him, "on the contrary, I feel better than ever."

As she spoke, her eyes remained on the sky. Her imagination was lost in the infinity of space.

Her ears caught the voices of the orphan girls joining the nuns in vespers. The organ murmured sounds like nasal voices singing the miserere.

"This singing reminds me of my childhood in the convent in Seville. This was the time of day I would pray with the most devotion... When I would leave the chapel, the fragrance of citrus blossoms in the orchard delighted my senses, and the last light of the sun sinking over the Guadalquivir saddened me so that I felt death very close at hand."

The doctor was not listening to Laura; like her, he was absorbed in imaginative contemplation: "Listen to that singing—such sweetness, such purity exists in those candid voices! Those sounds reveal the innocence of virgins intoning a prayer ...

"Listen... listen, Laura," the doctor insisted.

The song was faintly echoed by prayer, a pained murmur; it was a prayer for the dead.

"The Way of the Cross."

The sun had disappeared, but daylight lingered, melancholy like a *clair de lune*.

Chapter XIV

Between Laura and the doctor, the most earnest and cordial happiness prevailed. He said that he felt young again. Laura's garments served as his costume. Sometimes he played with her hat, or pretended to inhale the perfume of the roses adorning it; other times he wrapped his head in the veil, and the clinical instruments lost their solemn aspect, completing the jest of improvised, mischievous costumes. Once it happened that Laura was lying down, ready for her treatment, when the doctor came over and suddenly lifted her up, carrying her around the room as if soothing a newborn baby.

Laura protested, feigning anger, to which her lover replied: "A doctor is obligated to know his patient's weight; I am fulfilling my professional duty."

***

The methodical doctor systematically organized his life such that he saw Laura twice weekly.

One night he would go to Laura's house, and she would go to the clinic by day, at sundown, when all the clients had left. The hours spent at Laura's house were most desired by both; amidst silk, lace, flowers, and perfumes, the lovers' caresses sensed a propitious ambiance.

***

Laura was accustomed to removing her clothing at her dressing table before going to bed; then she would appear wrapped in a silk crepe kimono in pink or very pale sky blue, which formed a harmonic floral palette with bedroom lights softened by shades in muted tones.

One night, not wishing to interrupt the conversation in which they were engaged, Laura absent-mindedly began to undress in front of her lover, which produced in him such visible discomfort that he could not hold back from saying: "Please, don't undress in front of me, just think that in my clinic all the patients do the same. You can't imagine how that disagreeable sight haunts me, nor the concerted effort required to push it away."

Without replying, Laura hurried off for a brief moment, returning covered in a thick plush dressing gown that left not even her throat exposed.

"No, not like that," the doctor said, reaching out to her from the bed where he lay. "You may show your nude body, Laura, it's a marvelous work of art."

At that moment, he turned the electrical switch and illuminated the dim room, allowing him to observe Laura's pallor and the sad impression that his words had caused her.

Believing he had injured his lover's exquisite sensibilities, that night the doctor was intentionally more affectionate than usual; he renewed his caresses with the vehemence of the first night, seemingly insatiable in the pleasure of love.

Laura responded with the greatest tenderness, but without ardor; she was languid and she gave herself softly.

In her brain, an idea that had been torturing her soul for some time was taking resolute hold. She thought of the futility of her efforts, of the unevenness of the fight she was waging, and she felt lost, cruelly lost, lost in love.

Her beauty was visibly diminishing, while her illness was growing and devouring her like a pestilent, carnivorous reptile, draining her blood; in vain she had put all the warmth of her soul into play: her most seductive charms, the most exquisite refinements of subtle coquetry that emerged from this beautiful ailing woman in her dying youth, like the last fleeting flower of autumn. She sensed in the unfathomable collapse of her dreams that the moment of defeat was approaching, that the horrible disease with its brutal ugliness would triumph over all beauty, over every conception of art, burying her love, not with the destructive gloom of tragedy, but with that cold, lingering agony of abandonment that glimpses death without overtaking it.

She was convinced that the kind doctor's willingness always to sacrifice himself had prevented him from showing the force with which the spectacle of diseased matter pursued him, haunted his mind. Passion caused him to forget for but a few hours, perhaps a few months with short intervals, and now the tenacious, indelible reality was reappearing.

The sorrowful mourner, pilgrim of tenderness, sculptor of chimeras would have given anything to erase the spectacle of her past from her lover's imagination! Those hours of treatment, during which she had lavished him with charm and talent to distract him and conceal the ugliness of her disease, now caused her greater remorse than a Magdalene repenting for her sins. Oh, to forget! Oh, to tear out one's memory, make the past disappear, erase visual impressions, cleansing them with tears, numbing them with the throbbing of a turtledove!

The salvation of her love consisted of oblivion, of impossibility. How could he forget, this man of open eyes, who saw every day the mirror image of the love bed's nudity in the snow-white clinic?

***

Laura had always had the premonition that in their amorous union, the doctor was overcoming some instinctive repugnance; that he was making an effort to control himself and prevent her from sensing his discomfort. For long months she fostered in vain the hope that she could be fully cured; the inexorable disease alarmed her with distressing insistence; nevertheless, her primary focus was endeavoring to conceal within the depths of her body the stabbing pain that was tearing apart her insides and her soul, with the power to disenchant or disappoint her lover.

Fearful, greedy for his affection, she weighed her words, avoiding any moan or lament that could alert the doctor and prompt a separation. She was convinced that he would sacrifice his love for his duty; she knew his selflessness, strength, and resolve.

Chapter XV

The doctor easily grew accustomed to viewing Laura as a lover rather than a patient.

His obligation to treat her dissolved in delicious, indolent abandon. The feminine arts of attraction and seduction temporarily captured him over any scruple. The kiss of love drowned out the voice of reason.

Laura was happy, completely happy; in the soft refuge of sensuous caresses, it seemed that life had a double charm, and thus in her spirit all reason went numb, so that even her traditional religious beliefs dissipated into a pearly ether of somnolence.

She couldn't imagine how she had managed to live the first years of her youth without ensconcing herself in the mantle of sweetness lavished upon her by her lover.

***

One spring night the young woman awaited her lover, clad in a lilac kimono embroidered with sky-blue chrysanthemums and golden chimeras; a waxen pallor intermittently washed over her face with the look of an opium smoker; inexorable physical and moral laxity overwhelmed her, bowing her shoulders like a virgin of sorrows; she sensed a lack of air in the room, and after a momentary crisis of difficult breathing, she opened the window and dropped some cushions on the balcony floor; she lay down upon them submissively, like a distraught *musume*.

She contemplated the cloudless blue firmament as she waited for the doctor's habitual arrival. A postman broke her trance, like a dialogue between the stars of the heavens and a star of flesh, a runaway star fallen to earth seeking an early grave.

By pneumatic letter, the doctor informed her that a seriously ill patient had prevented him from coming. Laura spent the whole night under the open sky, writhing in pain on the cushions like a wounded samurai. Thus the night passed, black as suicide, as torture, until clairvoyance illuminated her understanding, inducing a vague fear. At the cool of dawn she decided to retire to her bed. When she lay down, an abundant hemorrhage obliged her to remain immobile, her trembling legs extended, paralyzed, to contain the red stream staining her body, flooding her as though she had been viciously stabbed.

At that moment, between horrors of matter and tortures of the soul, Laura had a premonition of something very sad, of something infinitely melancholy, of the end, the conclusion, and a vague and immense notion of the unknown.

The illness, her enemy, had just reared its bloody head; it was impossible to go on hiding; imperious like royalty, it showed no clemency in its destructive fury; Laura was transformed from a queen to its servant. She must resign herself to physical subjection, but not to spiritual servitude; she renounced the realm of love, the castle of opalescent dwellings, and this voluntary relinquishment of her lover, by a suffering heart needing affection more than ever, represented an act of heroism. She was not resigned like a eucharistic lamb to meekly display the beautyless sacrifice of consumption, of ravaged human flesh.

Chapter XVI

For six days, the doctor had not seen his lover: "Feminine whims," he thought. "Since I didn't go to her house, now she doesn't want to come."

Laura gave a banal excuse for being unable to go to the clinic; the doctor reread this letter, and in spite of himself, his imagination turned to the recent memory of another message written during the time when the vibrant joy of love was inspiring them intensely.

They had conducted a rather unscholarly philosophical discussion in which the words "psychology" and "philosophy" were interrupted by noisy kisses. They reached the conclusion that man, aside from his psyche, was a hot animal, and this definition caused them such hilarity that Laura would sign some of her written epistles by sending her regards to the hot animal.

After six days of absence, the beloved woman existed in his imagination only as something remote and delightful, fading in a vision of Renaissance silks and plush Oriental carpets, pearls and incense.

As he reflected, the doctor was walking briskly along the street to the home of a seriously ill patient ... Oh, duty, professional rigor, the terrible rival that had so often displeased Laura! Once again it came between the lovers, distancing them.

That night, there was no time for a bite to eat; the case was dangerous and it kept him for a long time by the side of his patient, who was perishing in agony. The physician fought tenaciously; the greater the severity, the more determined he became in his effort to save the man, more impassioned than a gambler.

The battle raged on, spirited and unyielding, between the will of the doctor and implacable death. From time to time, the shape of his lover's seductive body—a vision of gauze, perfume, and floating golden tresses—passed before the dying patient's bed, pulling the doctor away from the picture of agony that electrified his nerves with indescribable emotion.

A new summer day of pleasant recollections dawned for the doctor, who was able to leave satisfied, convinced that the patient had escaped death. Nostalgic melancholy soon overcame his spirits. Why was the memory of Laura taking intangible form?

No longer was she the disquieting woman of tempting power, whose black eyes seemed to be consumed by their own flame, but rather, something like a superhuman apparition, an illusion of legend, a heroine from the works of Hoffmann.

Chapter XVII

Somewhat calmed after managing to resurrect his patient, the doctor began to grow concerned by Laura's prolonged absence, counting the days and weeks; it seemed impossible that so much time had passed, and he was preparing to go see her when he received the following letter from a sanatorium in Berlin.

***

Leopoldo,

A soul that may have entered eternal life by the time you receive these lines begins her goodbye by asking for your forgiveness. Forgive me for hiding so much from you, and for preferring in my womanly vanity to die abroad, far from you, rather than leave you with the image of my mutilated, wrecked body associated with the memory of our love. I have said nothing to you of the physical pains that have come over me during our hours of love; the improvement I always spoke of was a lie, as were my happiness and laughter. Only my love was true, and the only indestructible thing was this passion, so intense that it burns my soul and overflows from my chest, such that the world would seem a small audience to hear me proclaim it.

I wanted my love to brighten your existence, for my youthful soul like a fragrant incarnate flower to delight your eyes, weary of the sight of suffering; but today, as my adverse destiny transforms me from an astonishing Venus —as you used to call me— into sad hospital waste, annihilated and exhausted, I prefer to run away, to distance myself from you and thus await my death... at least I will leave you the memory of the mysterious woman of the Bosphorus, 'with tresses of seagrass and eyes of the Oriental night,' and not the painful picture of my dying moments amid bandages, chloroform, and bloody scalpels. In Berlin, death causes me less sorrow; it is a city suitable for dying, as one leaves it behind without missing life; in Paris, in our opulent bedroom like a sultana's boudoir, it would have been sadder for me to die. I did not wish for funereal gloom to tarnish that room where our souls dwelled in a retreat of fervent love. A premonition, a superstition, perhaps, has been telling me for some time now that I am to die.

Do you remember that first afternoon of love we spent in your clinic? You heard the singing from the convent next door and commented on the virginal sound of the singing voices. I heard the prayer for the dead, and in the distance, I thought I saw the hazy shape of my mother waving, calling to me. The god Hymen did not crown our bed with roses. The nuptial music was a miserere, and the distant vision of the revered shade was a death omen ... Our love was grand, intense, capable of blotting out every premonition, every superstition; in our eagerness for life, it made us forget and cast off all reason and we experienced infinite pleasure; but death never left our side, for I was carrying it hidden within my being.

Goodbye! Will I ever see you again? I know nothing, and I have no hopes. Across the intricate mysteries of eternity, of the unknown, of the infinite, look for me, and I will wait for you always, if I exist always; but ask first if I look beautiful. If your spirit is weary of the spectacle of diseased nudes, and you wish to remember me, go to the studio of the painter X.; having always painted clothed women burning with sensuality, he painted my nude portrait with the mastery of his unmatched brush. Do not be shocked; it is a chaste nude. It will be the most perfect Venus of contemporary art, the painter insists.

My compatriot, Dr. Barrios, is by my side, and I have tasked him with bringing you the news of my death as soon as it occurs. Goodbye!... I love you so!...

***

The moment Dr. Castel's reddened eyes reached the end of the letter, his exhausted body fell into an armchair and he stammered, "Poor girl, poor little thing!," and his words were choked with sobs.

The doctor was in his bedroom at home. The shutters were open wide, providing a view of the Bois de Boulogne park in its somber late-summer green. The light of the waning sun was a flickering flame, like sparks of a fading lamp in the distance. From behind the trees it illuminated the foliage until it sweetly fell away. A sickly light enveloped the room in an ambiance of tortured gloom. The doctor stood and wordlessly contemplated the landscape where all was dying with the end of summer, the end of the evening, of the light, of the sun, and also of his love, as proven by the letter he brought to his lips with trembling hands. "The pain must be eternal, it will never end," he told himself, such was the force of his suffering.

***

A male servant came to interrupt his daze. He said that the gentleman who had brought the letter was Dr. Barrios, who had just arrived from Berlin and wished to see him; at the same time, Dr. Barrios entered the room.

The two men shook hands firmly without speaking, tears in their eyes. Dr. Castel spoke first: "How is this possible? ... Without me? No, it can't be true, Doctor, Laura isn't dead."

Dr. Barrios's silence spoke to the contrary, along with the tears he intermittently dabbed with a handkerchief.

After a few seconds of sorrowful silence, he began to speak:

"That was how she wanted it, sir. It was her will; only the day before her operation she gave me her confidence and the letter I delivered.

"It was impossible to avoid surgery. The fibroids had taken on large proportions of late, causing very heavy hemorrhaging, which returned at the time of the operation, so that there was no hope. The surgeons lost their minds, and poor Laura died. They considered opening up her abdomen for an ovariectomy, but it was too late. Besides, she had forbidden it. 'I do not want you to harm my body; if I survive, I want no trace as a reminder of the disease.' If she had wanted to have surgery in France, perhaps her fate would have been different. We would have foreseen, predicted what could happen; we were familiar with her nature, and that secret warning, that conviction she had that she was going to die, would have been reason for us to redouble our precautions..."

Dr. Barrios sighed sorrowfully, blew his nose loudly, and continued:

"When they applied the chloroform, she held a bouquet of violets in her hands and said to me: "Carnival time in Nice is so lovely!," and as she fell asleep, she let it go.

"I saved it for you, sir, even though it wilted."

"She didn't forget the violets," said Dr. Castel. "When she was alive, she gave me a fresh bouquet of them, with dewdrops trembling on the little petals, and their perfume intoxicated my soul with joy," and with this new remembrance of departed pleasure never to return, his eyes welled up with tears.

Their sorrow swelled for a few moments, the sound of sobs drowning out the echo of his voice, and the Spanish doctor continued: "Those were her last words...

"Poor Laura!—dying young and beautiful. It seemed death had been lying in wait for her. Some time ago, in the clinic, she said to me: 'Doctor, dogs howl in the night, heralding my death.'

"And before I left Paris, an owl came to my balcony from the church next door. Everything was foretelling her death, even the most insignificant omens. Death robbed her of life, but not of beauty. How beautiful she looked, like a statue of Carrara marble! Sculptors came to model her Grecian profile, her hands and feet, and a painter portrayed her in white tulle and lilies like a celestial virgin. Contrasting with the pallor of her face, her sardonic smile still seemed to say: I belong to the blue, to the intangible, I have left the Carnival of life!"

Dr. Castel was listening to him lethargically, overcome by the unspeakable sorrow of a secret regret.

"How could I forget her illness," he exclaimed in anguish, "my excessive love is what killed her!"

Chapter XVIII

The servant returned: "A client is looking for the doctor, he says his daughter is seriously ill and he's requesting a visit tonight."

To this, he replied with great indifference, for the first time in his career: "Tell him I'm out, and that you'll look for me," and he went on as though speaking to himself: "Not today, tomorrow, tomorrow... who knows when? How foolishly humanity insists on clinging to a life so cruel!"

And then he spoke no more; he sank into the armchair and his lips blushed red like a Sevillian carnation and his eyes, the brown of a Carmelite monk's habit, gave off flames of perdition, of infernal torment.

***

The Spanish doctor had sent for medicine from the pharmacy, and he insisted his friend take the drug, to no avail.

***

The darkness of night had long since penetrated the room where the two friends remained, one without the courage to leave, and the other fearful of being alone.

Unseen in the dim room, they were immobile like two sorrowful shades, and lingering in their midst was the image of death.

Sonorous laughter, sharp like birdsong, rang out, startling them.

"Can it be," the voice said, pushing the electrical button, "that you two are in the dark?"

The speaker was Dr. Castel's daughter, an exquisite 18-year-old girl. Her beauty had developed with Oriental luxuriance; she was blossoming with youth and joy.

Her cheeks glowed more intensely as she greeted Dr. Barrios. She extended her hand timidly. His eyes indicated that she should watch her father, as he said: "He isn't well; he needs the care of an affectionate daughter like you, miss."

The girl noticed her father's state of prostration and she was so moved by the painful expression on his face that, without a word, she put her arms around his neck, covered him with kisses, and burst into loud sobs.

"Life is sad, my dear," he said, stroking her hair.

***

Dr. Barrios went slowly on his way, thinking of the sensitivity and beauty of his colleague's daughter, and of the similarity between life and a rose garden: no sooner does one rose lose its petals and cease to perfume one man's existence, but a new bud opens into a new blossom, just as intense as that dead rose before it.

THE END

CPSIA information can be obtained
at www.ICGtesting.com
Printed in the USA
LVHW011345120519
617538LV00002B/260/P